Chapter 1

"Morning, Jill," Luther Stone said.

"Luther?" I'd been practising my 'surprised' voice for the last twenty minutes while I waited to ambush—I mean—bump into him. "I didn't see you there."

Luther Stone was my new neighbour. He was also my new accountant. He was also smoking hot.

"Just off to work?" he said.

He was so close I could have reached out and touched those firm biceps.

"Jill?"

Whoops. Daydreaming again.

"Sorry, I was miles away. Yeah, I'm just off to the office. What about you—what time do you start?"

"My first appointment isn't until nine-thirty this morning. I'm glad I bumped into you though."

Me too. We were obviously destined to be together.

"I've been thinking," he said.

Yes, yes, take me I'm yours.

"About the monthly review of your books."

"Huh?"

"You remember you wanted to keep on with the monthly review of your books rather than the quarterly ones which I suggested?"

"Yes. I'd prefer you monthly—to go over the books, I mean."

"Yes, well. It occurred to me that as we live in the same block of flats, it might make sense to do the review here."

"Here?"

"Yes. I've got all of your records on computer now, so it would be just as easy to do it here as at your office. If

that's convenient to you of course?"
"Convenient? Oh, yes, it's very convenient. I'm not doing anything else that night."
"I didn't actually mention a day."
Oh bum.
"Err—didn't you? Right, sorry."
"I was thinking maybe Thursday."
"Thursday? Let me think." Did I have anything planned on Thursday? Who cared? If I did, I would cancel it for Luscious Luther. "Thursday's fine. Your place or mine?"
"My place is still a bit of a mess after the move. I'll come to you if that's okay. How does eight o'clock sound?"
Like music to my ears. "Eight should be fine."
"Great. See you then."
I was so excited that I drove straight over to tell my sister, Kathy, my news.

She was wearing her pyjamas when she answered the door; she looked half asleep.
"What are you doing here?"
"Charming. I thought you'd be pleased to see me."
"I am always ecstatic to see you, Jill. Now, what are you doing here?"
"Where are the kids?"
"Pete dropped them off at school on his way to work. I'd just gone back to bed."
"Whoops, sorry. Did I wake you?"
"Yes."
"I have news."
"It had better be important."
"Can I come in?"
She sighed. "Only if you put the kettle on."

Kathy slumped on the sofa while I made us both a cup of tea. At least I'd be sure to get the right amount of sugar — one and two-thirds spoonfuls. I began to rifle through the cupboards.

"Where are the custard creams?"

"In the tin."

"No, I mean *my* custard creams."

"Oh, sorry. I didn't realise you meant *your* custard creams. They're in the tin too."

She'd done it on purpose. "I thought we'd agreed that you'd keep some separate for me."

"Yeah well, there was a slight problem with that plan."

"What's that?"

"I couldn't be bothered."

Even my sister's selfishness couldn't put a damper on my spirits. I had a date with Luscious Luther, and all was well with the world.

Kathy dunked a ginger nut into her tea.

"Do you have to do that?" I looked away.

"Lovely, soggy ginger nuts. Want a bite?" She waved the offending biscuit under my nose.

"You're gross. I hope you don't let the kids see you do that."

"We have biscuit dunking lessons every Friday. Anyway, what's so important that you dragged me out of my lovely, warm bed?"

"I've got a date." I paused for effect. "With Luther!"

What do you mean delusional? He'd asked me out hadn't he? He was coming over to my place, wasn't he? What was that if it wasn't a date?

"Luther the smoking hot accountant?"

"The very same."

"Wow! I didn't see that coming. When did he ask you?"

"Just now."

"Are you sure you were awake at the time? It could have been a dream."

"I'm sure. I just happened to bump into him in the corridor—"

"Happened to?"

"Purely by chance."

"Hmm."

"He's coming around to my place on Thursday."

"Good for you. It's about time you got back in the game. I guess Jack had his chance and blew it."

"Jack who?" I grinned. I was so over him.

"You're not planning to cook for Luther, are you?"

"I thought I would."

"Think again. That will be the last you see of him."

"I can cook."

"Baked beans on toast is not cooking."

Much as I hated to admit it, Kathy was right. I daren't risk scaring Luther off on our first ever date.

"You could come around and cook for us."

She laughed. "Yes, because I don't have anything better to do."

"Exactly."

"I was kidding."

"No, I think it could work. I wouldn't tell him you're my sister though."

"Oh?"

"I could tell him you're my maid."

Kathy spat out a mouthful of tea. "I am not pretending to be your maid, and I am not going to cook for you and your hot accountant."

"I suppose I could order in catering."

"That won't be cheap."

"What other choice do I have if my own sister won't help me out? Anyway, how come you look so rough this morning?"

"Nice of you not to mention it."

"Is Grandma running you into the ground?"

My grandmother had recently opened a yarn shop, Ever A Wool Moment, in Washbridge, and she'd given Kathy a job there.

"No, your grandmother is a little darling."

Grandma may be many things, but a 'little darling' she most certainly was not.

"If it's not Grandma over-working you, what is it? Are you sickening for something?"

"It's our new neighbour."

"I didn't know you had one."

"I did tell you, but as usual you weren't listening. Too busy daydreaming over Luther no doubt."

"What's wrong with them?"

Kathy stifled a yawn and shrugged.

"There's all kinds of strange noises coming from round there."

"What? Like loud music?"

"No, not music. Just weird noises. Pete said it sounded like howling."

"Have you met them yet?"

"It's not a 'them'; it's a 'he'. At least as far as we can make out. That's weird too. We didn't actually see him move in—no removals van or anything."

"It might have happened while you were out at work."

"Yeah, I guess."

"But you haven't actually seen him?"

"No. Pete went around there —"

"To complain about the noise?"

"No, just to say 'hi'. It was while I was putting the kids to bed. The noises hadn't started then. But anyway, whoever lives there didn't answer the door. Pete said he was sure there was someone in though."

"Weird. I thought I was the one with all of the strange neighbours."

"Except Luther, of course." Kathy grinned.

The sound of his name brought a smile back to my face. "Except Luther."

"Anyhow," Kathy said through yet another yawn. "Not to be rude or anything, but isn't it time you were going?"

Not to be rude? "I thought you'd want to hear my news. You're always going on at me to find a guy."

"Yeah, and I'm very pleased for you. Look!" She waved her hands in the air. "Big whoop! But now, I need to go back to bed."

"Aren't you in work today?"

"No, it's my day off. Now are you going, or do I have to throw you out?"

***

It was too early to go into the office, so I stopped off at a new coffee shop which had only recently opened. The Coffee Triangle was around the corner from Ever A Wool Moment.

The decor was very unusual, and I couldn't work out what the theme was supposed to be, but I noticed there were maracas on every table.

"Morning!" The young man behind the counter greeted me with a shake of his maracas.

"Err — morning."

"Beautiful morning." Another shake of the maracas.

"Err, yeah. Very nice."

"What can I get for you?" He shook the maracas a little too close to my face for comfort.

"Can I get a caramel latte, please? Regular."

"One caramel latte coming up."

"I like the Spanish theme," I said when he eventually got around to making the drink.

"It's actually not a Spanish theme."

"Oh, right. I just thought — with the maracas and all."

He reached under the counter, produced a triangle, and gave it a pleasing little strike. "The theme is percussion." He looked around, as though checking the coast was clear. "It's the boss's idea. Between you and me, I think it's a bit over the top. He's very into percussion. Today is maracas day. Yesterday was the tambourine, and tomorrow it's the xylophone."

"That's very — err — different."

"It can get a bit much when the place is full. Fridays are the worst."

"Drums?"

"Gongs. I tell you my head was pounding by the time I'd finished my shift."

I grabbed a copy of the Bugle, Washbridge's inglorious tabloid, and sat at a window seat. After a quick shake of the maracas — I couldn't resist — I checked the front page headline: It's Murder!

The article was another thinly veiled attack on the Washbridge police. Apparently, there had been two murders the previous day—it appeared they were unrelated. According to the Bugle, this was indicative of the general lawlessness which plagued the city. With two murders on his patch, Detective Jack Maxwell was going to be a busy man. He and I had a rather unusual relationship. When he'd first moved to the area, he'd given me a particularly hard time. Our relationship had subsequently improved, and the last time I'd seen him he'd suggested he might cook a meal for me. But that was a while ago, and I hadn't heard from him for some time. We certainly weren't an item—despite the best efforts of Kathy to push us together. And besides, I now had Luscious Luther, so it looked as though Jack had missed his opportunity. You snooze, you lose.

I finished my coffee, had a last shake of the maracas, and then left, but not before making a mental note to avoid Wednesdays (drums), Fridays (gong) and Sundays (triangle). What? I know triangles aren't loud, but I've had an irrational fear of them ever since that incident at primary school. I don't like to talk about it.

As I approached Ever A Wool Moment, I noticed the shop next door was boarded up. For as long as I could remember, it had been a fishing tackle shop: Rod's Rods. As far as I was aware, it was the only shop in the city which catered to Washbridge's anglers. Maybe Rod had retired, or maybe he'd relocated. So why was I getting bad vibes?

Grandma had invested heavily in LED signage for the shop since last I'd been past. In the centre of the window was a scrolling sign which conveyed the message: Never run out of wool again - Everlasting Wool is here! To the left was a smaller, but no less garish sign which scrolled the message: Throw away all those needles - One-sized needles are here! The third sign promoted the recently opened web site: EverAWoolMoment.com which offered one hour delivery anywhere in the country.

I could feel a migraine coming on just watching them all. I was about to turn away when I noticed the main sign change its message. It now read: *Shouldn't you be practising your spells instead of gawking at this window?*

Grandma! Did that woman miss anything?

Chapter 2

I was pleased to see the giant sign for Armitage, Armitage, Armitage and Poole had been removed over the weekend. It had been replaced by a much more modest one which did not completely obscure mine, as the previous one had done. I now shared the building with the AAA&P solicitors who also had the building next door. Gordon Armitage was desperate to get me out so they could have the whole building to themselves. That was never going to happen. Armitage had tried a number of underhanded tricks to dislodge me, but to no avail.

"Why are you wearing a hat?" I said.

Mrs V looked up from her knitting.

"My ears look old."

Mrs V was my PA/receptionist—unpaid. And before you accuse me of being a tightwad, I should explain that she did this quite voluntarily. I didn't feel too bad about it for two reasons: one—I didn't make enough money to pay her anyway, and two—she spent most of the day knitting.

"Aren't your ears the same age as the rest of you?"

"Oh no, dear," she said. "They're much older."

"Couldn't you just grow your hair?"

"It doesn't suit me long."

"It's a nice hat. Did you knit it?"

"Me?" She laughed. "I don't knit hats—you should know that. Scarves and socks are more than enough for me. Tulip Carruthers made it for me."

"Tulip?"

"Yes, she and her sister, Hyacinth, are the last word in hats. I could ask them to knit one for you if you like?"

"No, it's okay. I'm not really a hat person."

"Just wait until your ears get old, then you'll change your mind."

"How's Winky?"

Mrs V gave me a look, and I immediately regretted asking. Winky was my one-eyed, crazy cat who I'd rescued from the cat home. He and Mrs V were sworn enemies.

"He laughed at me," she said.

"Cats can't laugh."

"I know, but that's what it sounded like. When I went into your office to get a file, he made this weird noise. I could have sworn he was laughing."

"Maybe he's coming down with something?"

"Have you seen that crazy old coot out there?" Winky was rolling about the floor in hysterics.

"Shh!" I pushed the door closed behind me. Fortunately, Mrs V's hearing wasn't up to scratch—probably the old ears. "You shouldn't laugh at her. She's an old lady."

He could barely speak for laughing. "What's that on her head?"

"I like it. I think it suits her."

"You're such a bad liar."

"She has a problem with her ears."

"Are they falling off?" He sat up—suddenly more serious. "Hey, do you think they've fallen off?"

"Her ears? Course not—don't be stupid."

"She might be a zombie. Their ears fall off."

"Mrs V is not a zombie."

"It would explain a lot."

Did other people have this type of conversation, or was it

just me?

The door opened behind me.

"Watch out!" Winky yelled. "Zombie attack!"

I gave him a nudge with my foot—okay maybe more than just a nudge—which sent him sliding under the leather sofa.

"There's someone to see you," Mrs V said. "She doesn't have an appointment."

I had no appointments that morning, or afternoon, or for the rest of the week for that matter. As always, the punters weren't exactly beating a path to my door.

"Show her in. What's her name?"

"Miss Comm."

Miss Comm was in her late twenties, and as cute as a button.

"Thank you for seeing me." She managed a smile, but there was sadness in her eyes.

"No problem. Take a seat, Miss Comm."

"Dorothy, but everyone calls me Dot."

Dot Comm? I wanted to laugh, but I could see she wasn't in the mood for my stupid sense of humour.

"How can I help, Dot?"

"My fiancé is Ron Peel. His sister was murdered a few days ago. The police have arrested Ron on suspicion of her murder."

The name 'Peel' rang a bell. It was one of the murders I'd seen reported in the Bugle that morning.

"Where is he now?"

"At Washbridge police station. He was arrested last night, and they won't let me see him."

"What happened exactly?"

"I don't know the details, but Gina—that's his sister—was found murdered in an apartment over at the East Side Development. Do you know it?"

I nodded. What had once been a beautiful area of woodland had been cleared for executive apartments. Despite local opposition, the development had been given the green light—there had been rumours of corruption.

"Were your fiancé and his sister close?"

"Not really. They didn't see one another very often."

"Do you know why the police arrested him?"

"I assume it has to do with the money. Ron used to have a twin brother, Reg."

Ron and Reg? Someone was having a laugh.

"Reg died just over two years ago in a climbing accident. The two of them had been climbing together when Reg fell to his death. The terms of their parents' Will provided for all three children, but left the bulk of the estate to the last surviving child."

"So Ron is now set to inherit the estate?"

"That's right. As far as I can make out, that's the only reason the police have arrested him."

"Did you know his sister or his brother?"

She looked down as though contemplating her answer. When she met my gaze again, there were tears in her eyes. "I didn't know Gina very well. We'd only met a few times." She took a deep breath. "I used to go out with Reg. We had planned to marry."

"I'm sorry."

"After his death, Ron and I turned to one another for comfort. After a while that developed into something more."

"Do you have any thoughts on who might have murdered

Gina?"

She shook her head. "I really didn't know her very well. I met her a few times when I was with Reg, and no more than a couple of times since Ron and I got together."

I spent another twenty minutes gathering what other information I could from Dot, and I agreed to take on the case.

She'd no sooner left than Winky came rolling out from under the sofa.

"How did you do it?" He laughed.

"Do what?"

"Keep a straight face."

"I've told you. I don't find Mrs V's hat funny." I lied.

"I don't mean old crazy's hat. I mean that woman's name. Dot Comm? What were her parents thinking?"

"Making fun of people's names is not clever." And obviously something I would never do.

"Fancy another game of darts?" Winky pointed to the dart board which he'd had installed above the sofa.

"No thanks."

I'd been hustled by him once before to the tune of ten pounds. I wasn't going to fall for that one again.

"Go on. I'll give you a start."

"No."

"I'll play with two darts to your three."

"No, thanks."

"I'll play blindfolded."

"I'm too busy to play darts. I have a case to work on."

Mrs V caught me on the way out.

"Does Peter go fishing?"

"Occasionally, but not as often as he used to."

Peter was my long-suffering brother-in-law.

"I thought so. Tell him to be on the look out. I heard on the woolvine that there have been a lot of conmen targeting anglers. I wouldn't want him to get swindled."

"What kind of conmen?"

"I don't know exactly, but apparently they pretend to be something they're not. Tell him to be on the look out, and to tell any of his fishing buddies."

"I'll do that. Thanks."

I was about to head over to East Side when my phone rang. It was Jack Maxwell

"You've seen the Bugle, I take it?" he said.

"Two murders. That should keep you busy."

"Maybe I should get Susan back down here to help out."

Susan 'Sushi' Shay had worked with Jack before he moved to Washbridge, and she'd moved down here for a short while during which time she'd been the bane of my life.

"You should. I'm missing Sushi."

"I bet you are." He laughed. "Anyway, I promised you a meal."

"I thought you'd forgotten."

"Of course not. I've just been busy. Anyway, I came to the conclusion that if I wait until I'm not busy, I'll be waiting forever."

"Where did you have in mind?"

"I promised that I'd cook. Remember?"

"I thought that was a joke. Do you mean to tell me you really can cook?"

"I told you. I'm red hot in the kitchen. So what do you say?"

I probably should have mentioned that Luther and I were now an item, but I didn't want to hurt his feelings. And besides, I didn't want to jeopardise our fragile professional relationship. "Okay, when did you have in mind?"

"Friday would be best for me."

"Friday it is then."

Look at me. Two dates in one week. Was I hot or what?

"Jack, before you go. I ought to tell you that I've taken on a case related to one of the murders."

"I might have known. Which one?"

"The Gina Peel murder. The fiancée of the man you've charged came to see me."

"He hasn't been charged. We're just questioning him."

"Can you tell me anything?"

"What do you think?"

"I think 'yes'."

"Try again."

"Nothing at all?"

"I can tell you this much. There's something weird going on with the fingerprints. Look, I have to go. See you on Friday."

"Hang on!"

Too late. He'd gone. How could he leave me hanging like that? What did he mean by *something weird with the fingerprints*? Now I really was intrigued. If Maxwell wouldn't tell me then an 'undercover' visit to the police station was called for.

***

My cousins, Amber and Pearl, ran Cuppy C which was a cake shop and tea room. Like me, they were level two witches. Neither of them seemed particularly interested in moving up the levels. They were far more interested in Cuppy C and their fiancés, Alan and William.

"That's new isn't it?" I pointed to the sign on the wall above the counter.

"Yeah," Pearl said. "What do you think?"

The sign read: *'If our cupcakes don't make you happy, we'll give you another one'.*

"It's a nice touch, and I guess you don't have much to worry about—your cupcakes are the best in Candlefield."

"Yeah, that's what we figured."

"Jill, hi." Amber walked through from the cake shop. She was followed by four other young witches.

"Hi. I was just commenting on your new sign."

"The Cuppy C guarantee of satisfaction? Yeah, it's one of our better ideas." She glanced back at the four witches. "These are the friends of ours which we told you about. Ladies, this is our cousin, and P.I. extraordinaire."

Pearl joined us; we had to push two tables together to accommodate everyone.

"I'll let the girls introduce themselves," Amber said.

"Hi, I'm Tilly," the redhead with the tight braids, said.

"I'm Milly." The blonde to her right.

"I'm Lily." The tallest of the four.

Tilly, Milly and Lily? Was this a wind up?

"And I'm Hilary," said the one with a tiny tattoo of a butterfly on her neck.

"Let me guess." I grinned. "Everyone calls you Hilly?"

"No." She looked puzzled. "Everyone calls me Hilary."

"I just thought: Tilly, Milly, Lily. That you'd be—err—never mind. Anyway, I'm Jilly—err—I mean Jill. Jill Gooder. How can I help you?"

Chapter 3

It turned out that the four young witches ran a human/witch dating agency called 'Love Spell'.

"Where is it based?" I asked.

"We have two offices." Hilary seemed to have been appointed spokeswoman. "One here in Candlefield and one in Washbridge."

"Is it for any kind of sup?"

"No. It's for witches only. Witches who want to find a husband in the human world."

Now I understood why they had the two offices.

"But, isn't that a little awkward? I mean humans aren't supposed to know sups exist."

"The witches who sign up with us all know the rules. If they find a partner they're committed to keeping their 'secret' for life."

"What about the Washbridge office?"

"As far as the humans are concerned, we're just another dating agency. To keep our cover, we accept men and women. All of the women are matched with humans, but the more suitable men are matched with our witches."

"How do you decide which men are suitable to be matched with a witch?"

"It's difficult to put into words. It's more a feeling than anything else." The other three all nodded. "Some men just feel right."

"Sounds great. How long have you been in business?"

"Almost five years now, and going from strength to strength. Until six months ago."

Tilly, who up until now had said very little, chimed in. "It's sabotage."

"We don't know that for sure," Milly said.

"What else could it be?"

"What happened six months ago?" I said.

The girls all began to have their say, and I slowly managed to assemble their story. Their business had been going great guns until a few months ago when suddenly something strange happened. They'd kept meticulous records, and knew the percentage of introductions which would normally result in a successful relationship. That figure had barely changed over the time the agency had been in operation. If anything, it had improved slightly as the girls had become more experienced at making the perfect match. Then six months ago, the success rate plummeted. More and more introductions were leading nowhere.

At this point in the discussion, things became heated for a while. It was obvious to me that the two girls based in Candlefield, Tilly and Lily, blamed the two based in Washbridge, and vice versa.

"What are your fees?" Hilary said. "Since things started to go wrong, our income has taken a knock. We can barely pay ourselves a wage."

"Look, seeing as you are friends of Amber and Pearl, I'll take on the case on the basis that if I uncover anything, and things go back to how they were, you can pay me out of the additional income. How does that sound?"

There I went again—a sucker if ever there was one—no wonder I couldn't even afford to pay my own staff.

"That's very fair."

"See," Amber said. "Didn't I tell you our cousin was the best?"

***

How very strange! Usually when I went upstairs to my room above Cuppy C, I could guarantee that Barry would come running to me. But there was no sign of him. Maybe the twins had taken him around to Aunt Lucy's?

Barry was a Labradoodle, and the softest thing you were ever likely to meet. I adored him, but I would have been the first to admit he wasn't the brightest button.

Then I spotted his tail — sticking out from under my bed.

I knelt down and looked underneath.

"Barry?"

"I'm not here." He had his eyes closed.

"I can see you."

"No you can't. I can't see you."

"What's wrong?"

"I'm hiding."

"Why are you hiding?"

"Don't want the snap."

"Why don't you come out and tell me what you're talking about."

"Not coming out. Don't want the snap."

If he didn't want to come out, I probably wasn't going to get him out. Barry was a big dog — a big soft dog it's true, but big nonetheless. I had no idea what he was going on about, but he'd obviously got a bee in his bonnet about something.

The Love Spell girls had left when I went back downstairs.

"Thanks for agreeing to help them," Amber said.

"No problem."

"You should sign up with them, Jill," Pearl said.

"I'll have you know that I have not *one*, but *two* dates this week. With two different guys."

"Wow! Are you seeing Drake again?"

"No, both dates are with humans."

"Traitor." Pearl laughed. "Who are the lucky men?"

"Jack Maxwell—"

"Isn't he the policeman?"

"That's the guy. He's cooking a meal for me. And then I'm entertaining the luscious Luther."

"He sounds hot," Amber said. "Who's he?"

"He's my—err—he moved into my block of flats recently."

"You have to let us know how you get on," Pearl said. "My money is on Luscious Luther."

***

"Aunt Lucy!" I called as I let myself into her house. I'd knocked, but there had been no response. "Aunt Lucy!"

I could hear sounds coming from the dining room, so I made my way over there. "Aunt Lucy!"

"Do you have to make so much noise?" Grandma was sitting at the head of the table. Sitting with her, were five other witches, all old and all ugly. What? It's true! It looked like a convention for the ugly sisters.

"Sorry, Grandma. I was looking for Aunt Lucy."

There was a pot of money on the table, and the witches were all holding playing cards.

"She went out with Fester."

I resisted the urge to correct her. She knew full well Aunt Lucy's boyfriend was called Lester. She'd only said it to wind me up.

"Do you know when she'll be back?"

Grandma managed a shrug. "Do you want to buy in?"

I was sorely tempted. I could see they were playing poker—a game my adoptive father had taught me. He'd occasionally allowed me to join him on his monthly poker game. He'd put up my buy-in, and we'd split the winnings. Truth be known, I fancied myself as a bit of a card sharp.

"No, I don't think so."

"Are you chicken?" Grandma said—the other witches cackled.

"I have things to do."

"Cluck, cluck cluck." Grandma taunted me. That woman knew just how to press my buttons. Well I'd show her. She and her ugly friends would be laughing on the other side of their faces when I walked out with all of their money.

It's like riding a bike. You never lose it. I called, bluffed and generally played them into the ground. Three hours later, and the only two people who still had cash were me and Grandma. The others were still around the table—cheering Grandma on.

One hand, I'd take the pot, and the next, she'd take it back.

"I'd better get going," I said.

"One last hand." Grandma was already dealing the cards.

"Okay, but this is definitely the last one."

Jack of diamonds and king of spades. A mediocre hand, but I bet anyway. Grandma called.

On the flop came a three of hearts, six of diamonds and the jack of clubs. I had a pair, so bet again. Grandma called again.

King of diamonds came on the turn. Now I had two pair. Not bad. I bet again—bigger this time. Grandma called again.

King of clubs came on the river. I had a full house. I forced myself to think about ice cream because I didn't want Grandma to read my mind, and find out what cards I had. The twins and I had used the 'ice cream' ploy once before. I bet small—I wanted to tempt her in.

Grandma raised me. Bingo! I had her. I went all in. She called.

Yeah baby! I threw my cards face up onto the table. "Full house!"

I reached out and began to collect the cash when her bony fingers grabbed my hand.

"Not so fast, missy!" She turned her cards over. "Four of a kind!"

No! It wasn't possible.

Grandma scooped up the money while cackling to herself. "Thanks for the game, Jill," she said. "Any time you want a rematch, let me know."

I stomped out of the house without a word. I didn't trust myself to say anything to her.

***

I was back at my flat. I needed ginger beer and custard creams, and I needed them now.

Thirty minutes later, and I was still fuming. What were the chances of her getting four of a kind? I could still see the look on her face when she threw the cards on the table. I could still see those cards. Hold on! Just wait a minute.

They were jacks — four of them!

"You conniving little witch!"

She'd used magic to cheat me. I'd had two jacks in my hand, so how could she have had another four?

When would I ever learn?

***

I was still seething when I woke the next morning. What kind of grandmother would cheat her granddaughter out of her money? I had to find a way to get one up on her for a change. Yeah — like that was ever going to happen.

I was still intrigued by Jack Maxwell's comment about the fingerprints. What was so strange about them? He'd made it clear he wasn't prepared to share the information, so that left me with only one choice. I had to get inside the police station and find out for myself.

It wouldn't be the first time I'd done it. When I'd been hired to investigate the so-called 'Animal' serial killer, I'd used the 'invisible' spell to get inside. It had worked, but there'd been a few close calls when the spell had worn off. Whenever I thought of that, I remembered my close-up of Jack Maxwell's Tweety-pie socks. This time around, I was going to employ a different approach. I was a more experienced witch now, and I had more spells in my arsenal. Nothing could possibly go wrong this time.

***

"Oh no!" I scurried across the floor with the cat in hot pursuit. There was a small hole in the skirting board, but the wall was still a few metres away. The cat was getting closer; I could hear its paws pounding on the floor behind me. I slid the last few inches into the hole.

Phew, made it!

The cat was lying on his side, poking his paw into the hole. Fortunately for me, I was too far back for him to reach. Now, I knew how a mouse felt.

When I'd cast the 'shrink' spell, it hadn't occurred to me there might be a cat in the police station. I'd been expecting dogs, but had assumed they'd be on a lead or caged. What on earth was a cat doing there? Wasn't it against some kind of Health and Safety regulation? I had a good mind to report them. But right now, I had more pressing concerns. Like how to get out of this hole without becoming a cat's lunch. If I'd had the presence of mind, I could have reversed the spell as soon as the cat appeared, but blind terror had taken hold, and I'd been too busy running for my life. Anyway, even if I had reversed the spell, that would have landed me in a whole lot of different trouble. I was in one of the conference rooms on the first floor of Washbridge police station—how would I have explained my very sudden appearance?

So, I was in a hole—literally. Nice work, Jill. There was only one thing to do in a situation like this.

Chapter 4

No, I didn't mean I should eat a custard cream. Anyway, where was I supposed to find a custard cream in a mousehole?

I meant that I should ask myself: 'what would Grandma do now?' Much as I loathed the bossy, obnoxious, card-cheating old hag, I couldn't deny that she was one smart and powerful witch. So, what would Grandma have done if she'd found herself in this situation? Then it dawned on me—she never would have landed herself in this situation in the first place.

Was it my imagination, or was the cat's paw getting closer? I couldn't get any further away; my back was already up against the wall. If that feline managed to squeeze his paw any further inside, I'd be a goner.

I'd used the 'illusion' spell numerous times, so I felt confident with it, but I didn't know if it would work on an animal. I was about to find out.

Yes! It worked! Did this girl have skillz or what?

The cat hightailed it across the room and out of the door. He hadn't liked the look of the Pit Bull Terrier, which I'd conjured up. Not one little bit.

The room was filling up, and the conversations were getting louder. I remained in the hole which was at the front of the room—very close to the desk under which I'd hidden the last time I was there.

"Okay, guys!" The familiar voice of Jack Maxwell came from my left. I was relieved to see him push the door closed behind him. At least I didn't have to worry about the cat coming back.

"I'm going to keep this brief," he said, as he walked over

to the desk. He was no more than a few feet away from me now.

Oh no! What was it with this guy and his cartoon-themed socks? Had there been a fire sale? Today he'd gone for Roadrunner. How was anyone meant to take him seriously when he insisted on wearing those?

"Okay," he said. "A quick recap first. There were two murders over the weekend. As far as we are aware there is no connection between them, which is why I've set up two separate teams. I'll lead the investigation into the murder of Gina Peel, and Detective Chalmers will head the investigation into the murder of Anton Michaels. Depending on how things develop, we may need to swap resources around. For now, I want Jimmy, Graham, Stevie, Angie and Carla to work on the Michaels case. Get yourselves over to conference room five. Chalmers is already in there."

Maxwell waited until they'd left, and then continued. "Gina Peel was found dead in an apartment in East Side. It wasn't her apartment—we're still trying to trace the owner. She'd been stabbed—the murder weapon was found in the property. Forensics have lifted finger prints from the knife, and from the apartment. The good news is we have a match; the bad news is they match a certain Reginald Peel."

"Is that the guy we have in custody?" someone called out.

"No. The man we are questioning is Ronald Peel. He's the brother of the victim. Reginald Peel was Ronald's twin brother. There's just one minor complication—" Maxwell paused. "Reginald Peel died two years ago in a climbing accident."

Wow! No wonder Maxwell had told me there were

complications regarding the fingerprints. If I'd understood him correctly, the man they were interviewing, my client's fiancé, was not the man whose fingerprints they'd lifted. They belonged to his twin brother who died two years ago.

The remainder of the meeting was taken up with Maxwell assigning duties to his team, after which the room cleared. Once I was sure the coast was clear, I crept out of the mousehole. After the close shave with the cat, I felt very vulnerable at my minuscule size. It had been a hairy journey into the building—avoiding all the giant feet. I was too exhausted to do it again. I needed a way to pass through the building without attracting any attention, and I thought I knew just how to do it.

It was great to be back to full size. Now I was becoming more adept at magic, I was able to get much more out of spells than I had before. Many spells were available in more than one flavour. When I first started to use magic, I'd always settled for the basic, default options. Now I was more confident, I felt able to be more creative. For example with the 'doppelgänger' spell which I'd just cast. The default version affected only the person you were looking at. However there was an option which meant everyone you encountered would be affected. This took way more focus, but that came much easier to me now.

I walked along the corridor, and no one gave me a second glance. A couple more minutes, and I'd be out of the building and home free.

"Susan?" Jack Maxwell said.

Whoops! The one person I hadn't wanted to bump into.

"What are you doing here?" He had a puzzled look on his

face.

Hardly surprising because he thought he was looking at Detective Susan Shay (or Sushi as I'd come to know her). I'd figured no one would give Sue Shay a second glance. No one except Jack Maxwell.

"Jack." I tried to mimic the mannerisms of Shay by running a hand through what Jack saw as my curly, peroxide blonde hair.

"I didn't know you were down here."

"Just a flying visit. I left a couple of things behind: straightening tongues, bleach—that sort of thing. I thought I'd better come and get them."

What? I'm allowed to be bitchy—she deserved it.

"How long are you down here for?"

"Just a few hours. I promised Toby I'd be back tonight."

"Toby?"

"Didn't I mention Toby? He and I have become very close." I gave him a sexy wink.

"Have you got something in your eye?"

"Look, I'd better get going."

"Okay. Nice to see you again."

"And you." I made to turn away, but then hesitated. "Oh, and by the way. I think I may have misjudged that P.I. What was her name? Jill? She really is very talented."

If only I'd had a camera to capture the expression on Maxwell's face. Gobsmacked didn't even come close.

***

I was still smiling to myself when I got back to the office. Mrs V had what looked like a brand new laptop on her desk—what was going on? Mrs V didn't *do* computers.

But even more strange—she wasn't knitting. In fact there wasn't a knitting needle or ball of wool to be seen. Instead her fingers were going nineteen to the dozen over the keyboard.

"Mrs V?"

"Morning, Jill." She checked her watch. "Afternoon, I mean."

I ignored her wisecrack. "New computer?"

"Yes, I got it with Yarn Stitches."

"Sorry?"

"It's a bit like Air Miles, but for yarn. I've been saving them for years, but there wasn't anything which caught my eye until now."

"You must have had a lot of points—I mean stitches—to get that."

Not that I was any kind of expert, but the laptop looked like a high-end model.

"I had just over two million."

"Wow! But then, you do get through an awful lot of wool."

"Not so much now that I have the Everlasting Wool subscription. Did I tell you I've upgraded my plan to give me five colours a month?"

"Grandma will be pleased."

"That reminds me. Your grandma called in this morning. She asked me to give you a message, but to be honest it doesn't make a lot of sense."

"What did she say?"

"Well at first, I thought she was talking about that detective friend of yours, Jack Maxwell, but then she said 'six jacks are better than four'."

I could gleefully strangle that woman.

"Do you know what she was talking about?" Mrs V said.

"I think so. It's nothing to worry about. Just Grandma and her little joke." I took a deep breath. I wouldn't let that woman get to me. "Anyway, why did you get the laptop? Are you writing your memoirs?" I laughed.

"No, but I am writing a book. It's called 'Scarf knitting for complete thickos'."

"Hmm. The title may need a rethink. Only dummies would class themselves as 'complete thickos'."

"You might be right. How about V for Knitting? Like V for Victory."

"Again, I see a minor flaw. Maybe give it some more thought?"

"You're right. I'm sure I'll come up with something."

Winky was on the window sill.

"Have you seen what the crazy old bag lady is up to now?" he greeted me.

"I do wish you wouldn't call her that."

"Have you seen her though? She's writing a book."

"What's wrong with that?"

"Who's going to buy a book written by that headcase?"

"Mrs V is a well respected figure in the world of yarn. I'm sure there'll be a lot of demand for her book."

"You have to say that because no one else would work for you for free. Can you spell EXPLOITATION?"

"Hold on. I'm not exploiting anyone. Mrs V does it out of the kindness of her heart."

"Tell that to the Bugle when they get hold of the story. I can see the headlines now: Well known P.I. refuses to pay staff! Read all about it."

"The Bugle wouldn't be interested in that."

"Maybe." He smirked. "Maybe not. But if someone was to email their news desk—anonymously of course—who knows what might happen?"

"You wouldn't."

"I could be persuaded not to."

"Salmon?"

"Red?"

"Obviously."

I gave him the salmon, but I still didn't entirely trust him.

"Mrs V, sorry to interrupt your flow."

"That's all right, dear. What about 'Where there's a wool, there's a way' for a title?"

"Too contrived. You need something short and snappy."

"Hmm."

"Would you contact Dot Comm to set up a meeting, please? Oh, and one other thing, if you get a call from the Bugle, tell them 'no comment'."

"About what?"

"Anything. Just tell them 'no comment' and hang up."

***

Tomorrow was 'L' day. 'L' for Luther. 'L' for luscious. I had to pull out all the stops, and that included a new outfit. Something alluring, something sultry, something which said, 'come and take me. I'm yours'. There were other things I probably should have been doing—like background research into the Peel family. But to heck with that—I was a woman on a mission.

If I hadn't been daydreaming about Luther, I might have

spotted Betty Longbottom, my tax inspector neighbour, before I bumped into her. She wasn't alone.

"Jill, hi." Betty beamed. Betty didn't usually beam.

"Hi, I didn't see you there."

There was something familiar about the young man standing next to Betty, but I couldn't quite put my finger on it. I felt like I knew him from somewhere.

"This is Norman," Betty said.

Norman! Of course. Or mastermind, as I would always think of him. I'd first met Norman when I was investigating a murder at Washbridge Amdram. Norman worked in his uncle's prop shop. When I'd tried to question him about the props, he'd famously told me he didn't know 'owt about owt.'

"We've already met," I said.

I looked at Norman. Betty looked at Norman. Norman looked out to lunch—as per usual.

"Do you know Jill?" Betty asked him.

He opened his mouth, and for a moment I thought he was going to come out with the classic line, but instead he managed only, "'Huh?"

"We met at your uncle's shop. You probably won't remember."

He didn't. He probably didn't remember his name most days.

"How did you two meet?" I asked.

Betty beamed even more; Norman obviously had hidden depths. "Through the personal ads in Sea Shell Monthly, didn't we Norman?"

Norman nodded.

"So, do you collect sea shells too, Norman?" See, I can make small talk when I try.

"No. I collect bottle tops."

"Right. I see." I didn't, and Betty could tell.

"Norman's a bit short-sighted, aren't you?"

He nodded.

"He's also a bit forgetful. He'd gone out without his glasses, and stopped off to buy a magazine. He'd intended to pick up Bottle Tops Monthly, but picked up Sea Shell Monthly by mistake."

"An easy mistake to make."

"Anyway, he had a browse through it, and found my details in the personal ads. I guess that's fate for you."

"That's amazing. Well, I'd better press on. I have one or two things to get."

"Bye!" Betty said.

"Who was she?" Norman said.

***

It had taken the best part of two hours, but I was thrilled with my purchase. You can't go far wrong with a little black number—or so I'd read somewhere. I'd also invested heavily in candles—got to set the right mood. Tomorrow night couldn't come around quickly enough. This was going to be the start of my great, romantic adventure. I could feel it in my blood.

Chapter 5

The next morning, I phoned Mrs V to tell her I wouldn't
be going into the office.

"Will you feed Winky, please?"

"If I must."

"Don't forget, it's—"

"Full cream milk. I know." I could hear her sigh. "Jill, I
think I may have come up with a title for the book:
'Scarves are from Mars, Socks are from Jupiter'. What do
you think?"

"Someone beat you to it. Keep trying."

It was my date with Luther tonight. The day ahead would
have been perfect had it not been for my magic lesson
with Grandma. I didn't look forward to those at the best
of times, but after the rotten trick she'd played on me at
the poker table, I really didn't want to see that woman.

I'd arranged to meet the twins at Aunt Lucy's house. It
had been a while since I'd seen her. I arrived early, and
there was no answer when I knocked on the door. I turned
the handle, and as usual it was unlocked.

As soon as I stepped inside, I heard footsteps on the
landing. I glanced up just in time to catch a glimpse of
Lester. He was hurrying towards the bathroom—wearing
only shorts and a vest.

"Jill?" Aunt Lucy appeared at the kitchen door.

"Morning. I hope you don't mind me calling by so early."

"No—err—of course not. Come in." Was it my
imagination or was she a little more flustered than usual?

"Did I catch you in the middle of something?"

"Me? No. Come in. I was—err—Lester is coming around

later. I was just tidying up."

Huh? Lester was coming around later? Was that the same Lester I'd just seen dive into the bathroom, I wondered?

"Lester?" I said.

"Yes. He's coming around in a little while. Most probably after you and the girls have gone to practise."

I couldn't help but smile. Aunt Lucy was blushing.

"Hi, Mum!"

"Hiya, Mum!"

The twins had arrived.

"Jill!" Pearl gave me a hug. "You're keen this morning."

"I'm not." Amber pulled a face. "I don't know why we have to have these stupid lessons. It's not like we want to move up to the next level. One of our staff has called in sick. We should be at Cuppy C."

That was the first time I'd heard either girl admit they weren't interested in moving up levels, although I'd long suspected it. Even though I shared their dislike of Grandma's lessons, I was keen to go as far as I could with my magic.

"I suppose we'd better get a move on." Pearl sighed. "Grandma's meeting us there."

"We heard that Grandma won all of your money at poker," Pearl said, as we made our way to the Range.

"Who told you?"

"Grandma. Who do you think? She was boasting about how good a card player she is."

"She cheated. She blatantly cheated. I should have won."

"You should tell her that," Amber said.

"Are you trying to get Jill killed?" Pearl scolded her sister.

"It's time we all stood up to her," I said.

The twins stopped, looked at me earnestly for the longest moment, and then laughed.

"I'm serious. We shouldn't let her walk all over us like this."

"I don't know what you're complaining about," Amber said. "You've only had a few months of this to put up with. We've had her around all of our lives."

"You both deserve a medal."

They giggled.

"There's something else, but I'm not sure if I should mention it," I began.

"You have to now," Pearl said.

"Yes, spill the beans. We love juicy gossip."

"When I got to Aunt Lucy's just before you two arrived, I saw —" I shook my head. "No, I really shouldn't say. It's none of my business."

The twins exchanged a glance.

"You mean Lester?" Amber blurted out.

"You know?"

"Of course we know. He's been more or less living there for almost a week now. Mum doesn't think we know, but we're not stupid."

"I'm surprised you haven't said anything to her."

"This is way more fun." Pearl giggled again. "When we're around there, and we know he's hiding upstairs, we ask Mum where he is, and watch her splutter as she tries to come up with some story or other."

"The best one yet was when I said I wanted to go up to our old room to look for something. I thought Mum was going to have a seizure." Amber laughed. "She said the room had been fumigated, and we weren't allowed in."

"You two are cruel!"

***

"What's tickling you three?" Grandma met us at the gates to the Range.

"Nothing, Grandma," we chorused.

"Do you usually laugh at nothing? They'll be locking you away. Now if you were laughing at Jill's poker exploits, I might understand the hilarity."

I stopped laughing. Not satisfied with cheating, she now had the gall to rub my nose in it.

"You're not having much luck with *Jacks* of any kind, are you?" she quipped, and then cackled at her own joke. If ever I made level six, she would so get hers.

"Well at least you managed to bring a smile to her face," Pearl whispered as we made our way into the Range.

"She's been a real misery guts all week," Amber said.

"What's new?"

"She's been even worse than usual because of Ma Chivers."

"Who?" I asked.

"Hasn't Mum told you about Ma Chivers?" Amber glanced ahead at Grandma to make sure she wasn't listening.

"I've never heard of her."

"You're probably going to hear a lot about her from now on. Ma Chivers and Grandma progressed through the levels together initially, but Ma Chivers reached level six before Grandma. She won the Levels competition when she was only on level four. Not long afterwards, she moved to the human world. She's been gone for over a century, but now she's back to stay apparently. Grandma is not impressed because she's returned just in time for the 'Elite' competition."

"What's that?"

"It's an annual competition for level six witches only. The winner is awarded the Elite Cup."

"I bet Grandma always wins doesn't she?"

"She rarely takes part. She reckons she is above such things. Mum says Grandma used to win it every year, but she got tired of it because there was no meaningful opposition. Anyway, Ma Chivers has called her out—she said if Grandma doesn't show up for the competition, everyone will know she's afraid of her."

My curiosity was sparked. Since discovering my 'new' family, I had yet to see anyone come close to getting the better of Grandma. I wanted to meet this Ma Chivers.

"You really don't want to meet her," Grandma said. I'd done it again—I'd allowed myself to become complacent when I should have realised she'd be crawling around inside my head. "I know you think I can be a little unpleasant at times," Grandma said.

A little unpleasant? Just like the bubonic plague was a little unpleasant?

"But once you've met Ma Chivers, you'll change your mind. You'll think I'm the nicest person you've ever met."

The twins and I all exchanged a look, but said nothing. Anything we did say would no doubt be held against us in the court of Grandma.

"Quiet!" Grandma raised a crooked finger. We were in the Spell-Range. "Today's lesson will be on the 'jump' spell. "Which of you has memorised it?"

The twins shrugged in unison.

"I have," I said.

The twins mouthed, 'I have'. I ignored them.

"I might have known." Grandma produced two spell books out of thin air, and threw them at the twins. "You have ten minutes." She turned to me. "You, come with me."

I hadn't liked the look of the 'jump' spell when I'd read about it. Its innocent name hardly did it justice. When I first saw it, I'd assumed it would simply allow me to jump higher—big whoop. I'd been wrong. The spell effectively made your feet act as powerful springs—multi-directional springs. So, for example, if I was standing between two buildings, I could leap from one to the other, and back again in a kind of diagonal motion. Think parkour, but on steroids. On paper, that all sounded well and good, but in reality, I'd never been great at jumping. I always stepped over the line in the long jump, and crashed into the bar in the high jump. That did not bode well.

Grandma took me to the far side of the Range—to an area I hadn't seen before. Sure enough, there were two high brick walls which stood parallel to one another.

"I don't get this spell," I said.

"You don't get it? What's to get?"

"I know what it does, but I don't know why I would ever need to use it. Couldn't I just as easily use the 'levitate' spell?"

Grandma sighed at my apparent stupidity. "You'll never make a witch if you can't master the art of spell selection. As you progress up the levels you'll come across numerous spells which appear to overlap in terms of their functionality, but the key is recognising the right spell for the right situation. After 'focus', 'spell selection' is the most important thing for you to master. Take the 'levitation' and 'jump' spells for example. What is the main difference between them?"

I hated it when Grandma did a pop quiz. I invariably gave the wrong answer.

"Levitate lets you rise in a straight line. Jump lets you—err—bounce from side to side."

"*Bounce?*"

She knew full well what I meant.

"Apart from being able to *bounce* what else is different about them?"

I wished the twins were with me—at least then, they could have shared in the humiliation.

Then suddenly out of the blue, the answer came to me.

"The speed!"

"Better late than never. That's right—the speed. The 'levitation' spell has its uses, but if you're in a hurry then the 'jump' spell is much better.

No, no. I mustn't smile. Whatever I did—I mustn't smile.

"Something funny?" Grandma's wart was in my face.

"No."

"Do you usually smile for no reason?"

"No, sorry. I had an itchy nose."

If nothing else, I was getting better at scrambling my thoughts to stop Grandma reading them. Just as well too, or she'd have realised I was smiling at the idea of decrepit, old Grandma trying to use the 'jump' spell to bound up a wall.

I'd no sooner thought it than—

She leapt onto the first wall, and then bounced across to the second, and so on and so forth until she reached the top. Just as quickly, she made her way back to the ground in a similar fashion.

My flabber was well and truly gasted.

"You were saying, missy?"

The wart was back in my face. So much for my thought scrambling. I opened my mouth to speak, but couldn't find the words.

"When you've done catching flies, it's your turn."

I stepped forward so I was standing between the two walls. If Grandma could do it at her age, how difficult could it be? I took a deep breath, closed my eyes, cast the spell, and then leapt. Even though I'd seen Grandma do it only moments before, I was taken aback by the sheer force with which I left the ground. The trick was to glance off one wall towards the opposite one.

Thud!

I totally mistimed it, and instead of bouncing off the wall, I came sliding back down to earth.

"Impressive," Grandma cackled. "What do you call that?"

I had a sore knee, but the only thing really hurting was my pride. I pushed past Grandma and had another go — with the exact same result. Grandma made some comment, but I wasn't listening. I wasn't going to be defeated by some stupid level two spell.

The problem wasn't in casting the spell — that was working fine. It was in my timing. I had to focus on the timing. I leapt up again — this time I caught the first wall just right, and the second. Now I had the hang of it. Moments later I was sitting on top of the wall. I heard applause coming from below, and for one insane moment, I thought it was Grandma.

Yeah, right.

The twins had joined us and were waving to me.

"Nice one, Jill!" Amber shouted before being reprimanded by Grandma.

Getting back down was a breeze. I couldn't help the huge grin which was plastered across my face. Grandma looked as unimpressed as ever.

"Right," she said. "Now it's your turn." She turned to the twins who looked as terrified as one another.

"Those walls are really high," Amber said.

"And hard," Pearl added.

"Stop your whining and get moving. Which one of you wants to go first?"

Neither of them volunteered.

"In that case, you can go in alphabetical order."

Pearl sighed with relief.

"Reverse alphabetical order."

Chapter 6

After the lesson was over, I made my way to Aunt Lucy's while the twins hobbled back to Cuppy C.

Normally I'd have knocked on the door and walked in, but since the whole 'Lestergate' incident, I thought it best to wait until Aunt Lucy came to the door. I didn't want to cause embarrassment.

"Jill? Why didn't you come in?" Aunt Lucy said. "The door wasn't locked."

"Err — I — err."

"How did the lesson go today?"

"I thought it was okay, but I'm not sure the twins would agree."

"Oh, dear. What happened?"

"We were practising the 'jump' spell."

I saw Aunt Lucy cringe.

"I just about managed it okay, but Amber and Pearl — they have a few bruises."

"What was she thinking?"

I didn't need to ask who the 'she' was.

Aunt Lucy clenched her fists. "What's the point of her teaching that spell to those girls? They're never going to need it."

"I'm not sure I will."

"It's different for you. You need to have every spell in your arsenal because you have The Dark One to consider, and besides you'll need to master them all if you're to move up the levels."

"Who says I want to?"

"Don't you?"

She already knew the answer. I wanted to emulate the

achievements of my mother, and much as it pained me to say it, Grandma.

"I guess so."

"I don't know why she won't let the twins be. They're perfectly happy being on level two, and they already have all the magic they need to get by. It's not like either of them has shown any interest in moving into the human world permanently."

"Would that make a difference?"

"Oh, yes. So many things can go wrong in the human world. The more magic you have at your disposal, the better."

Aunt Lucy checked her watch.

"Look, I'm sorry, but I have an appointment in a few minutes." She hesitated. "With Miles Best."

"Have the twins found out that he's been selling your cakes?" I asked.

"No, thank goodness, but it's only a matter of time. I've already told the middleman I won't be making any more cakes for him."

"None?"

"No. I can't trust him not to pass on orders from Miles to me, so it's best I don't make any at all."

"Won't you miss the money?"

"I'll get by. I did before."

"If you've told the middleman you aren't going to work for him any longer, why do you need to see Miles?"

"He found out I was the one supplying the cakes. I think the middleman must have told him, and now he's threatening to tell the twins unless I continue to supply him."

"The scumbag!"

"I called him much worse than that when I found out. That's why I thought I'd better have a few choice words with the young man."

Although Aunt Lucy was not in the same class as Grandma when it came to 'scary', I still wouldn't have wanted to get on the wrong side of her. Miles Best might regret his actions before the day was over.

***

Why was I so nervous? I felt like a teenager on her first ever date. I checked my watch for the millionth time. Only a few more minutes and Luther would be here.

I ran through the check-list — again.

Sexy black dress — check.

Lights dimmed, candles strategically placed — check.

White wine — chilled.

Delicious cordon bleu meal prepared — check (with a little cheating, but we needn't get into that).

My mouth was dry, and my heart was racing.

There was a knock on the door.

"Did I get the wrong night?" Luther said.

He was dressed in jogging bottoms and a tee-shirt. A little informal, but I could still work with that.

"This is Lucinda. She's my trainee. I thought she could sit in on this session. But if I have the wrong night?"

Lucinda?

"Jill? Are you okay?" Luther looked concerned. "You look as though you're expecting someone for dinner."

"Err — yeah — I am. My — err — friend — pen friend. From Spain — err — or Italy. I haven't seen her — him in years."

"Oh, right. I'm sorry to have disturbed you then. I must have got my days mixed up. I'll give your P.A. a call to reschedule."

"Right—okay—thanks—bye!"

I closed the door and got the wine out of the ice bucket.

Some hours later, my phone rang.

"Jill? Are you okay?" Kathy said.

"Could wot be betta." Hiccup.

"Are you drunk?"

"No! I'm wot dronk."

"What happened? With Luther."

I laughed uncontrollably. "Luther has a loose sinder."

"A loose what?"

"Loo Sin Da. He was wearing jigging bottoms."

"You need to go to bed."

Hiccup. "Goo Niyt."

"Good Night."

***

Would someone please remove my head? I can manage without it for one day.

I crawled out of bed; I was still wearing my little black number—aargh. The memories came flooding back. The look on Luther's face when he saw me dressed to kill, and then again when he saw the candles. What had I been thinking? How had I managed to convince myself we were on a date? He was coming over to go through the books. How would I ever look him in the face again? I bet he and his trainee—what was her name? Lucinda? I bet they had a really good laugh. Why was I such an idiot?

And why was I wearing this stupid dress?

My phone rang—much too loudly.
"Kathy?"
She laughed. "Oh boy. You sound terrible."
"Thanks."
"I'm not surprised though. Not after last night."
"How do you know?"
"Don't you remember? I called you."
"You did?"
"Yeah. You weren't making much sense though. Something about jigging bottoms and a loose sinder."
Oh no. My embarrassment was complete.
"So, what happened?" She pressed. "I gather the date wasn't a runaway success."
"I don't want to talk about it."
"Come on. You know I'll keep at you until you do."
"Fine! Apparently I was the only one who thought it was a date. Luther, who I might add doesn't look nearly so luscious in jogging bottoms." It was a lie—he'd still looked really hot. "Luther turned up with his assistant—Lucinda."
"Why would he bring his assistant—" She laughed again. I hated my sister. "Oh, wait a minute. I get it now. He was coming over to look at your books, wasn't he?"
"He should have made it clearer."
"And you conjured up the whole date thing." She was laughing hysterically now.
"Gotta go. Very busy. Bye." I ended the call.
Rub salt in the wounds, why don't you? I might have known Kathy would be understanding—not.

***

I felt a little more alive once I'd showered and forced down some toast. I cracked the door open just wide enough to see down the corridor. I did not want to bump into Luther—ever again. The coast was clear, so I made a dash for it.

After the events of the previous night, the last thing I felt like doing was visiting a dating agency, but I'd promised to call in and see the girls at Love Spell. I planned to visit both of their offices today starting with the Candlefield branch.

The receptionist was a wizard named Daniel. He was a delight.

"Tilly and Lily are expecting you. Can I take your coat? What would you like to drink? I like what you've done with your hair."

"Thanks, Daniel," Tilly said, once he'd delivered me to a small meeting room.

"Nice to see you!" the parrot said.

"That's Sidney," Lily said, gesturing to the bird cage.

"Nice to see you!"

"Not one of Hilary's better ideas." Tilly sighed. "She thought that having a parrot in each office would put clients at their ease."

"Nice to see you!"

I tried to focus on what Tilly was saying, but it wasn't easy. "Does he say anything else?"

"Nice to see you!"

Tilly and Lily shook their heads. "There's a coffee shop next door. Do you want to go there?"

"Nice to see you!"

"That's better," Lily said as she brought over the coffees.

"Do you think the parrot might be responsible for the recent downswing?" I took a bite of a giant blueberry muffin. What? I'd heard they were good for hangovers.

"I'd like to blame it on Sidney." Tilly had chosen a raspberry muffin to match her hair. "But he's been on board from day one, so it can't be that."

"I might be speaking out of turn," I said. "But during our first meeting, I couldn't help but pick up a kind of 'us and them' vibe between the two offices."

The two girls nodded.

"You're right," Lily said. "It hasn't always been like that, but since things started to go wrong — well —"

"Look." Tilly took over. "The stats don't lie. The increased rate of failures has all been at the Washbridge end."

"I don't follow."

"The percentage of witches who have decided not to pursue the relationship has barely changed since we started. The problem is with the humans — the men. The percentage of them who have decided not to pursue the relationship after the initial date has increased dramatically."

"What do you think is happening?" I glanced down at the plate. Had I really eaten the muffin already? They must be making them smaller.

"We don't think they're vetting the applicants thoroughly enough. When we set up the business, we all agreed that the vetting process would be the key to our success or failure. Hilary and Milly must be letting anyone through. I don't see what else it can be."

"Have you mentioned this to them?"

"Of course, and it didn't go down well. They blamed us. They tried to say the men were only dropping out because we weren't maintaining standards at our end. Cheek! We only take on twenty percent of the witches who apply to us."

"As low as that? What determines if you accept someone?"

"There are lots of different factors, but primarily we have to make a judgement as to whether we think the witch would be capable of living in the human world."

It had never really occurred to me until then, but of course the couple would have to live in the human world.

"What about keeping the fact that she's a witch from her boyfriend or husband?"

"That's another important factor. Not every witch is capable of keeping her powers under wraps. We actually run courses to help with that though."

I was intrigued. "What kind of courses?"

"We cover all kinds of things. Things you might take for granted. As a witch it's easy to become reliant on your magical powers. In the human world, the witch must either learn how to use these discreetly or learn how to cope without. You wouldn't believe some of the applicants we see. We've had witches who have never made a meal without resorting to magic. Some of them use magic to make a cup of coffee."

Now why hadn't I thought of that? Not that I'd be so lazy — obviously.

Chapter 7

Back in Washbridge, I made my way to the other office of Love Spell. I noticed I had a couple of missed calls from Kathy, but she could wait. If I knew her, she'd have more jokes lined up at my expense. My 'date' with Luther was going to take some living down.

I was surprised to find Daniel, the wizard, on reception there too.

"Hello again, Daniel," I said.

"It's Nathaniel."

"Sorry?"

"My name. It's Nathaniel."

"Oh, sorry. I could have sworn—"

"Daniel's my brother. We're identical twins."

Daniel and Nathaniel—nice.

"I'm Jill Gooder. I have an appointment."

"Oh yes. Milly and Hilary are expecting you."

The Washbridge offices were more upmarket than their Candlefield counterpart. The girls were waiting for me in a meeting room at least twice the size of the one I'd been in earlier.

"Jill, thanks for coming," Milly said.

Hilary greeted me with a smile.

"Where's your parrot?" I asked, as I took my seat.

They grinned. "We gave up on that crazy idea a couple of weeks after we opened."

"Do the Candlefield girls know?"

"Now you come to mention it, we may have forgotten to tell them." They laughed.

Hilary and Milly told me pretty much the same story as I'd heard earlier.

"Look, if the problem is with your own vetting system, then I'm probably not going to be able to help."

"We understand that, but we thought if we could at least rule out outside interference, then we'd know the problem was internal."

"Is there anyone else you suspect of trying to damage your business?"

They both shook their heads.

"What about competitors? Any possibilities there?"

"It's a very specialist market as you might imagine. The only two competitors we have are: Charming and Enchanted," Milly said.

"And we have a great relationship with both of them. We all know one another, and we even socialise. I really can't believe it's something they'd do."

"Any disgruntled ex-employees?"

"None. There's only ever been the two of us in this office, and Tilly and Lily over at Candlefield. Plus Daniel and Nathaniel, of course."

"You're really not giving me much to go on."

"We did have one idea," Hilary said. "Why don't you sign up and test out the service? We'll easily be able to match someone as pretty as you."

Flattery would get her everywhere. And after the Luscious Luther debacle, I could use some help in the dating stakes.

"Okay. That sounds like a plan. Let's do it."

***

"Auntie Jill!" Mikey greeted me at the door. "I've got a rat."

"Yuk. Where?"

"It's in my bedroom. Do you want to come see?"

"Maybe later."

I'd made arrangements to pop around to Kathy's before the Luther incident. I was now regretting that decision—I knew she'd be merciless.

"Let Auntie Jill get through the door, Mikey. She can look at your rat later."

"Rat?" I screwed up my face. "You let him have a rat?"

"It's not his. It belongs to the school. The kids take turns taking it home for the night. The thing gives me the creeps—its eyes follow me whenever I go into his bedroom."

"Guess what I've made!" Lizzie shouted.

"What?" I felt I had to ask, but in all honesty, I didn't want to know. She and Kathy seemed to take great pleasure in tearing apart my beloved beanies, so they could create all kinds of hybrid freaks.

"A Tigrich." She beamed.

I looked to Kathy for a translation.

"Tiger, Ostrich, of course. A Tigrich."

Gross!

"Come and see." Lizzie dragged me into her bedroom. I could have wept. Lying all around the room were my darling beanie babies. The ones I'd collected, catalogued and kept in pristine condition for over a decade. And now? I couldn't bear to look at them.

"Look!" Lizzie thrust the monstrous thing into my hand. It had the body of a tiger and the neck and head of an ostrich. "It's a Tigrich. Guess what I call him?"

"Frank?"

"No. His name is Luther. Mum thought it up. It's a nice name, isn't it?"

"Fantastic!"

I heard Kathy laughing, and turned to find her standing in the doorway.

"Very funny!" I snarled

"Thought you'd like it. Come on through to the kitchen. I'll make you a cuppa while you tell me all about your date. I could do with a good laugh."

"How much sugar did you put in here?" I asked. It was ridiculously sweet.

"Two thousand, three hundred and thirty-six granules."

"You're hilarious."

"Talking of hilarious — tell me again what Luther said when you answered the door."

"Can we please drop the subject?"

"Like a *stone*?"

"Ha, ha. Anyway, there's something I need to tell you while I remember."

"Is this you trying to change the subject?"

"Yes, but I do actually have something to tell you. Does Pete still go fishing?"

"Occasionally. Probably a couple of times a month. Why?"

"According to Mrs V there are some conmen around who are targeting anglers. You'd better warn him to be on the look out."

"What's the scam?"

"I've no idea. Mrs V heard the news on the woolvine. It might be nothing."

"Auntie Jill!" Mikey pounced on my lap. "Come and see

the rat."

Before I could object, he'd dragged me by the hand into his bedroom.

"Look!" He pointed to the cage on top of his cupboard.

"What's his name?"

"Rat."

"No, I mean what do you call him?"

"Rat's his name. My teacher named him."

Just then, I heard Peter's voice. He was home from work.

"Dad!" Mikey shouted. I began to follow him to the door.

"Wait here, Auntie Jill. I'll be back in a minute."

"Okay." I sat on the bed.

And then it happened.

"Thank goodness for that!" the naked man said. "I needed to stretch my legs."

My mouth fell open.

"Whoops, sorry!" he said, grabbing a pillow to cover himself.

I looked at the empty cage, and then back at the man.

"You? It? Rat?" I prided myself on my articulation.

"Yeah. Rat the rat, that's me."

"Are you a wizard?" I said in a low voice. I can normally sense these things, but I wasn't sure with this guy.

"No. A shape-shifter."

"Like a werewolf?"

"I suppose. Werewolves are the poster boys of the shifter family. Rats—not so much."

"It must be horrible living in that cage."

"Are you kidding? It's the best gig I've ever had. Most of my friends are stuck down the sewers. I get to visit a different house almost every day. And the kids love to sneak me chocolate and stuff."

"How did you get out of the cage?"

"Nothing to it. Think about it. If I can change from a man to a rat, getting through those bars isn't really a problem."

"I guess not."

"How long have you—"

Without warning, the man dropped the pillow, and turned back into a rat.

"Jill?" Kathy said. "Why are you talking to the rat?"

***

The next day, I'd arranged a meeting with Dot Comm at her apartment. I hadn't expected to find her fiancé, Ron, there.

"Did the police release you without charge?" I asked him.

"What choice did they have? I've a good mind to sue them for wrongful arrest."

Dorothy took hold of his hand. They were sitting side by side on the sofa.

"Tell her the rest," Dot encouraged him.

"Nothing to tell," he grunted.

"Ron, please! She can help."

He shrugged. He was obviously a man of few words. Dot took up the story.

"Now they're saying he helped his brother to fake his own death."

Colour me confused. "I thought his brother died in a climbing accident?"

"He did. I should know," Dot said. "The whole thing is nonsense."

"How on earth did they ever come up with that theory?"

"It's because they found Reg's fingerprints in the apartment where Gina was murdered. They believe the twins faked Reg's death, and that he has actually been in hiding for the last two years. They think he came out of hiding to kill Gina, and now the twins plan to split the inheritance between them."

"That's too fantastical for words. Even if it was true, why wait for two years to kill Gina?"

"According to the police, it would have been too suspicious to have killed her shortly after Reg died."

"There's one way to prove it was actually Reg who died," I said. "And that's to exhume the body."

"No!" Ron shouted. "I won't allow it. Reg has been laid to rest and that's the way it's going to stay."

"But you could prove—" I began, but Ron wasn't in the mood to listen.

"I won't allow it. Reg stays where he is."

Dot showed me out of the apartment.

"What do you think will happen?" she said in a low voice.

"The police will probably insist on an exhumation regardless of what Ron says. It's the only way they'll know for sure who was actually buried there."

As I made my way on foot back to the office, I ran the case over in my mind. I could kind of follow the police's reasoning. It had been Reg's fingerprints which were found on the weapon that killed Gina Peel, and in the apartment where she was murdered. He could hardly have been there if he'd been buried two years earlier. If they could prove the body which was buried two years ago wasn't Reg Peel, they had the twins banged to rights.

I was a little concerned by Ron's reaction to the suggestion of an exhumation. Was he genuinely upset at the idea of disturbing his brother's remains, or did he have something to hide?

***

The shop next door to Ever A Wool Moment was boarded up. Rod's Rods was, to the best of my knowledge, Washbridge's oldest fishing tackle shop. According to Kathy, it was one of Peter's favourite shops—he could spend hours in there looking at flies—whatever floats your boat. He'd be devastated when he found out about the closure.

Just then, the door of the boarded-up shop opened, and a man sporting a baseball cap with the words 'Rod's Rods' on the front, emerged. He was carrying a large box. I could see he was struggling with the door, so being the Good Samaritan I am—not because I was being nosey, obviously—I grabbed the door for him.

"Thanks," he said.

"No problem. Any idea why they're closing?"

He put down the box which looked ridiculously heavy, and tried to catch his breath. *"They* is *me*. I'm Brian. I am— err—was—the owner."

"Brian?"

"Yeah. Brian's Rods didn't have the same ring to it. So I became Rod."

Made sense, I guessed.

"My brother-in-law will be sad to see you close shop. He loves his fishing."

"There'll be a few people sad to see the shop close."

"Are you retiring?"

"I guess so. I hadn't planned to, but my hand's been forced."

"Economic climate?"

"That hasn't helped, but it's more than that."

"Oh?"

"It's been one thing after another. First the shop was flooded. Then we had an infestation of rats. Then the power went out, and the energy company couldn't get it fixed — it came back on by itself in the end, but not before we'd lost several days trading. This is going to sound stupid, but it's almost as though the place is cursed."

"That's terrible. I'm sorry to hear that. How long has that been going on?"

"That's the weird thing. Everything was okay up until a few months ago, and then everything went pear-shaped."

He picked up the box.

"What will you do?" I asked.

"I'll be okay. I've put cash aside — guess I'll have time to actually do some fishing now. Thanks again for the help. Bye."

"Bye."

I took a step back, looked at the boarded up shop, and then glanced next door. How long had Ever A Wool Moment been open? I was getting bad vibes. Very bad vibes.

Chapter 8

Dinner with Jack Maxwell. I should have been more excited than I was, but I was still stinging from my encounter with Luther. And besides, I didn't totally trust Jack—I always had the feeling that he was trying to get one over on me—like with the bowling. Not that he'd ever manage it. Still, it had to be better than staying in my flat and moping. And it was certainly better than going over to Kathy's, and having her take the mickey.

It could prove to be an interesting evening because Jack had said he intended cooking dinner himself. Now it was perfectly possible that he was a good cook—many men are—although curiously, I'd yet to meet one. Somehow, he didn't strike me as the culinary type. He was more the 'fish, chips and mushy peas' type. Maybe I was being unfair—I was about to find out.

His flat was a fifteen minute drive from mine. I'd toyed with the idea of taking a taxi, but decided I preferred to have an excuse not to drink. I'd done with drink for a while after my post-Luther binge.

"Come in." Jack greeted me at the door with a welcoming smile. "You found it okay?"

"Yeah. I'm a P.I., remember."

"Dinner will be about thirty minutes. Care for a drink?"

"Just soda. I'm driving."

He led the way into the living room which had a minimalist feel to it.

"You have a lot of bowling trophies." I almost managed to say it without smirking. "Pity you missed out on that last one."

"Are you going to rub that in again?"

"Oh yes. Plenty more mileage left in that yet. Did you have to hire a separate van to transport these?" I ran my hand along the top of the trophy cabinet.

He smiled. "I'd better go and check on dinner. Have a seat."

"Why don't I give you a hand?"

"No!" He looked panic-stricken. "Sorry. I mean—No, it's okay. I got this. Take the weight off your feet. I'll only be a minute."

I didn't take a seat. Instead, I studied the various photographs which he had on display. One was of a couple in their fifties or sixties who I guessed were his parents. Another was of Jack and another man who looked like a slightly younger version of him—his brother, I assumed. There were several photos of Jack being awarded a trophy. Those bowling shirts really didn't do anything for him. I was pleased to find there weren't any photos of Susan 'Sushi' Shay or any other women come to that. Perhaps he'd hidden them away before I arrived.

When he wasn't being 'Detective Maxwell', Jack could be good company. I'd discovered that on our first so-called date—the one where Kathy had rigged the raffle. He was interesting and funny. And although he wasn't in the same league as Luther on the 'phew' scale, he was still pretty hot. Not that I'd noticed.

And he could cook. I mean really cook. The meal was one of the best I'd had for many a month. I'd been expecting fish fingers and chips with ice cream for dessert. Instead, I'd been treated to a culinary feast.

"Well," I said, after the last spoonful of lemon tart (to die for). "I have to say that was delicious. Thank you."

"You sound surprised." He grinned.

"I am a little."

"That's rather sexist."

"I suppose so. I haven't come across many men who know how to cook. Peter's not bad—"

"Peter?"

"My brother-in-law. But he's not in this league."

"Why thank you, kind lady."

Just then a phone rang. Maxwell took it from his pocket, checked the number, and said, "Sorry. This is urgent, I have to take it."

"Sure, no problem."

Whatever or whoever it was, he didn't want me to overhear, so he walked off in what I assumed was the direction of the bedroom.

A good looking guy who could make me laugh and could cook? Why was I wasting my time with Luther? Jack Maxwell seemed to have it all—even if he could be a bit of an asshat at times.

The sound made me jump. It had come from the kitchen. Jack's flat was on the ground floor. Had someone climbed in through the window? Jack was still in the bedroom, so was unlikely to have heard it. I'd better take a look.

"Gordon?"

"Jill?

Gordon Blare looked almost as surprised to see me as I was to see him. I'd hired Gordon a few nights earlier to prepare the meal I'd planned to share with Luther Stone. He was a cordon bleu chef who prepared meals for paying clients in their own homes. I hadn't trusted myself to cook a meal worthy of the evening I'd envisaged spending with Luther, so I'd hired Gordon.

"I didn't realise you were here," I said.

"Busted." He shrugged.

Maxwell had brought in a chef and intended to take credit for the meal himself. Despicable! What? Of course it's completely different to what I'd done. I'd fully intended telling Luther. Totally. Probably.

"Oh?"

I turned around to find a red-faced Jack Maxwell staring at us.

"You were going to let me think you'd made this yourself, weren't you?" I grinned.

He held his hands up. "Guilty as charged."

"Can you actually cook?"

He shook his head. "I do a mean beans on toast, but that's about it."

Gordon left, and Jack and I laughed it off. In some ways it came as a relief to know Jack was every bit as useless in the kitchen as I was.

Just as on our previous date, he was good company. Away from the job, Jack Maxwell was someone I really liked. And he seemed to like me too. The evening ended with goodbyes, and a peck on the cheek. Not very exciting granted, but maybe it was the start of something? Maybe.

***

It was Saturday morning, but I still had to drop in at the office—I had a cat to feed. Surely if Winky could talk, send messages by semaphore and fly a remote control helicopter, he could feed himself? But then, maybe that wasn't such a good idea because he would have been the size of a barrage balloon.

"Morning, Winky."

He didn't look up—he was too busy typing away on my computer. I'd told him not to use it and I'd changed the password a dozen times, but I was wasting my time. That cat could hack his way into anything.

"I hope you aren't ordering things, and paying for them with my credit card again."

"Shush! You're interrupting the artistic juices."

What was he up to now?

"Is that a new eye patch?"

"It is." He looked up. "What do you think?"

"I like it. The sequins work surprisingly well."

"That's what I thought. It's part of the new disco range. I bought a couple."

So he *was* using my credit card to buy goods again. No wonder my bill was always so high.

"Stop ordering stuff. I'm broke."

"Chill out. I'm not ordering anything. If you must know, I'm writing a book."

"You?"

"Why not? If the old bag lady can do it, then I'm sure I'll have no problem."

"What kind of book?"

"It's a fantasy/adventure."

"A novel?"

"Yeah, why not?"

"What's it about?"

"Before I tell you, I'll need you to sign this." He pushed several sheets of A4 paper across the desk.

"What's this?"

"Just an NDA."

"You want me to sign a Non-Disclosure Agreement?"

"It protects us both."

"Don't you trust me enough to take my word?"

He shook his head.

"Okay." My curiosity had got the better of me. "I'll sign your stupid NDA."

"On pages five, seven and ten."

I signed three times and passed it back to him.

"Right. So the plot is this: There's this young boy who finds out he's a wizard, and he goes to this school for wizards —"

"Hold on! That's already a thing."

"What is?"

"That story. It's already been done."

"Impossible. This was all my idea."

"I'm pretty sure someone got there first."

"Well, even if they did, it can't be as good as the book I'm going to write. I'll sell thousands — maybe even millions." He scratched his chin. "There's just one thing. I'm struggling for the main character's name."

"Harry?"

"Nah. I was thinking of something more along the lines of Bruce. 'Bruce and the Mysterious School for Wizards'."

"Catchy."

"Yeah — I thought so."

I was on my way out of the office when I got a call from the girls at Love Spell. Hilary confirmed they'd arranged a date for me with a human — it was scheduled for Thursday evening at a restaurant called Kaleidoscope — one of three restaurants they used for all first dates. If nothing else, I'd get a free meal out of it.

I'd promised to give the twins a hand in Cuppy C for a few hours. Now I knew the ropes, I actually quite enjoyed my time behind the counter. It made a change from the cut and thrust of being a P.I. After all, what could go wrong in a tea room?

"I asked for skinny," the disgruntled witch said.

"Sorry. I'll swap it."

"I asked for a single shot—this is way too strong." An unhappy werewolf complained.

"Sorry. I'll get you another."

"Jill, why don't you take a break?" Amber nudged me out of the way. A little disgruntled, I went over to join Pearl who was also on her break.

"I thought I'd got this tea-room lark cracked," I said.

Pearl laughed. "You might kick our asses at witchcraft, but you're pretty useless behind that counter."

"Gee thanks."

"It's okay. We like to have you around. It makes us realise how good we are. It would be horrible if you were better than us at everything."

"I guess." That didn't make me feel any better about being such a klutz.

"Did Amber tell you about the fancy dress competition?"

"No, but then we've never had a minute."

"It's a week on Sunday. You have to go."

"I don't think so." I'd never seen the point of fancy dress competitions.

"It will be a hoot. And there's a cruise for two for the winner."

Even I had to concede that was a pretty good prize, but not good enough to make me want to put myself through that kind of torture.

"What are you and Amber going to go as?"

"We haven't made our minds up yet, but we definitely aren't going to go as some kind of silly pair. Mum saw salt and pepper costumes, and said we should hire those. I'm not going to dress up as a condiment for anyone."

"If you win I assume you'll go on the cruise with Alan?"

"No. Amber and I have agreed if either of us wins, we'll go together."

There were times when I wondered why the twins had got engaged. It seemed to me they would come up with any excuse to leave their fiancés behind.

Amber had managed to get away from the counter, and she came over to join us.

"I've been telling Jill about the fancy dress," Pearl said.

"You totally have to go." Amber took a bite of the cookie she'd snagged from the counter.

"I hate fancy dress."

"You'll love it. Did Pearl tell you what the prize is?"

"Yeah. Still not interested. I'll come and cheer you two on though, if I can get away. By the way, how's Barry? Has he come out from under the bed yet?"

"He's over at Mum's house."

Chapter 9

Oh my! I have a new love in my life. No, not a man. I'm in love with Aunt Lucy's fruit scones, which are too delicious for words. I feel a little disloyal to my beloved blueberry muffins, and of course my custard creams, but right now all I want is a second scone.

"Help yourself to another if you like." She must have read my mind. No, seriously, knowing my family, she probably had.

"I shouldn't."

"Are you sure?"

"Well, go on then. They are rather small."

Aunt Lucy laughed. We both knew I'd just redefined the term 'small'.

"I'm glad you came over," she said. "There's something I wanted to talk to you about."

I nodded. I couldn't speak because my mouth was otherwise engaged with pure scone delight.

"It's about Barry."

Oh no. What had he done now? If she was going to tell me she and the twins could no longer look after him when I was in Washbridge, what would I do? I couldn't take him back with me.

"Look!" She pointed out of the window.

Barry was trying desperately to scale the wooden fence into the next garden. Not that he had any chance of doing so—it was at least six feet tall.

"What's the matter with him?" I said after I'd washed down the scone with a glass of milk.

"The neighbours have bought a lady dog. Barry seems rather keen to meet her."

"That's nice."

"Yes. Well it would be if he'd — " She lowered her voice as though Barry might actually hear us. "If he'd had the 'snip'."

"Snip? Oh, right. The snip." I screwed up my face at the thought of it. "That explains it."

Now it was Aunt Lucy's turn to look confused.

"Last time I was here, he wouldn't come out from under the bed. He kept going on about the 'snap'. I didn't have a clue what he was talking about."

"I think it's something you need to get sorted."

"Me?"

"He is your dog."

"Yeah, but — err — won't he hate me?"

"Probably, but not for long. Give it some thought."

I was going to try my best not to. Poor old Barry.

"How did your showdown with Miles Best go?" I asked in an attempt to take my mind off snipping.

"He wasn't *best* pleased." Aunt Lucy laughed at her own pun. "He said if I didn't continue to bake cakes for him he'd tell the twins that I'd been supplying them to him."

"But you didn't even know they were going to his shop."

"It's okay. I think I know how to convince him that threats won't get him anywhere." She gave me a knowing wink.

***

It was Monday morning, and I'd managed to get out of my block of flats without bumping into Luther again. I was about to set off for the office when my phone rang.

"Morning, Jack. You're bright and early."

"Don't say I never do you any favours. You're going to hear anyway, so I thought I'd let you know that an order has been granted to exhume Reginald Peel's body. Or at least whoever's body is buried there."

"Did Ron change his mind and agree to it?"

"No, but then we didn't need him to. Look, I have to go. I just wanted to say I enjoyed the other night."

"Me too. Even if you did lie through your teeth about who cooked the meal."

"You enjoyed it didn't you?"

"It was delicious, but I can't believe you'd stoop so low. I would never do anything like that." What? White lies don't count.

"Next time we'll dine out. How does that sound?"

"Sounds great."

"Right. Got to dash."

Now we'd find out why Ron Peel was so upset at the idea of disturbing his brother's remains.

***

Mrs V had abandoned the laptop and was back to knitting. At least, she would have been if she hadn't been so busy trying to control the three unruly men who were seated in the outer office. As soon as I walked through the door, they leapt to their feet.

"Sit down and wait!" Mrs V pointed a threatening knitting needle at them. "Stay!"

I gave Mrs V a puzzled look.

"These three *gentlemen* are all here to see you. They do *not* have an appointment."

"Miss Gooder, I'm Stephen—" One of them stood up.

"Sit down!" Mrs V gave him the evil eye.

He sat.

"Jill, can I have a word in your office?" Mrs V said.

Once in there, I said, "Who are they?"

"Publishers."

"Which publisher?"

"They aren't together. They're from three different publishing companies."

"Really? I suppose you'd better send them in."

"Separately?"

"Might as well get it all over with at once. Send them all in, would you?"

While Mrs V went to collect them, I looked around for Winky. He was usually on me as soon as I walked in the door—not because he was pleased to see me obviously, but because he wanted feeding. I spotted him under the sofa—staring at the three men who Mrs V had just ushered into my office. He was up to something, but I'd have to wait to find out what.

"Right gentlemen. Pull up a seat, and tell me what all the fuss is about."

They all began to talk at once.

"Whoa! Why don't you all introduce yourselves first? Left to right."

"I'm Peter Entwhistle and I represent Black Python Publishing."

"I'm Colin Malone and I represent White Arrow Publishing."

"And I'm Stephen Jefferson. I represent Blue Cocktail Publishing."

"So, it's not all black and white then?" I laughed at my own joke.

They didn't. They just shared a puzzled look. It was so difficult to find an audience for my sophisticated humour.

"What can I do for you gentlemen?" I said.

"I understand you are representing the author of the book which is being auctioned," Jefferson said.

The three of them shared a remarkably similar bad taste in ties, but Jefferson's just edged it.

"What book?"

"White Arrow is keen to make an offer."

"I think you'll find we have the better distribution, and will offer the best advance," Entwhistle said.

"Advances aren't everything," Jefferson interrupted. "We can offer the best royalties going forward."

Wow! I knew knitting was popular — what with Wool TV and all — but who'd have thought it was this popular? Mrs V was going to make a killing. I wished she'd warned me that she'd named me as her agent. I guess she thought I'd be better at dealing with hard-nosed businessmen like these.

"Gentlemen, gentlemen. You will all have an opportunity to put forward your offers, which I and my client will give careful consideration to. Before you do that though, maybe you should tell me what other wool publications you have in your stables?"

I'd succeeded in confusing them again. They looked at one another, and then back at me.

"Wool?" Malone said.

"Yes. My client will want to be sure you have experience in marketing books in the same genre."

"Well that's where we excel," Entwhistle said. "You've probably heard of the 'Joe the Wizard's school days' series of books."

"Really, Peter." Malone interrupted. "Are you trying to compare those to our, 'Edward the wizard's school adventures'?"

"Neither of those can hold a light to the, 'Paul the wizard does his homework' series," Jefferson said.

I glanced across at Winky who had a huge grin on his face.

"So let me get this straight. You gentlemen are all here today to bid for the right to publish the 'Bruce' book."

"Yes, indeed," Malone said. "Am I right in thinking that you represent the author, Win Key? Tell me is that Edwin or Edwina? The letter didn't make it clear."

"I'm afraid I'm not at liberty to give you any more details about the author. He or she is a very private person."

They all nodded their understanding.

"Look, gentlemen, no decision is going to be made here today. I'd like you to submit your offers to me in writing by the end of next week."

"But, Miss Gooder, if I could —"

I put my hand up to stop Malone mid-sentence.

"That's my final word. Best offers in writing by next Friday. Now if you don't mind, I have other business to attend to."

The three of them trailed out of the room. As soon as they'd gone, Winky leapt onto my desk.

"Forty per cent," I said.

"What?"

"That's my cut."

"In your dreams. Five per cent."

"Thirty."

"Ten."

"Twenty."

"Ten or I get the old bag lady to do it."
"Okay. Ten it is."

After I'd fed Winky, I had a few words with Mrs V.
"Who were those horrible men?"
"No one important. It's all dealt with now."
"I wasn't going to waste a perfectly good scarf on them. They were simply dreadful—no manners at all."
"How's your book coming along? I see you aren't writing today."
"I have something else on my mind at the moment. Wool TV have asked me to do my first ever studio interview for them."
"How exciting."
"I know. I'm really thrilled, but also very, very nervous."
"Who will you be interviewing?"
"That's just it. They won't tell me. They insist they want spontaneity. They don't want me to go in there with pre-set ideas or prepared questions."
"Wow! That really does sound scary."
"And what's even worse, is that it'll be going out live."
A recipe for disaster if ever there was one.
"I'll let you know when it's going to air as soon as I know."
"Yeah. That would be good."

***

I'd promised to meet Daze in Cuppy C. She wasn't in the tea room when I arrived, but Amber and Pearl were. They were both in tears of laughter.
"What's going on?"

Neither of them could speak, so they pointed out of the window.

Best Cakes owned by Miles Best and his girlfriend, Mindy Lowe, was directly across the street. I could see both of them inside their shop, but I couldn't for the life of me make out what they were doing. It would have been pointless asking the twins who were helpless with laughter.

I walked out of Cuppy C, and made my way across the road.

Then I started to laugh too.

Miles and Mindy were running around the shop, desperately trying to grab the cakes which were floating in the air. They were fighting a losing battle. The customers in Best Cakes were either looking on in disbelief or holding their sides from laughter.

Aunt Lucy — what a card!

Daze had arrived by the time I got back to Cuppy C. Amber had managed to compose herself enough to bring drinks and cakes to our table. The twins could see we were in conference, so didn't join us. The last time I'd seen Daze was to hand over the papers I'd managed to grab from Alicia's flat. Alicia Dawes was a level two witch who had poisoned me, and who I believed was working with The Dark One (TDO).

I've had my people go over the papers," Daze said. "There's little doubt that Alicia is working for, if not with, TDO."

"Are you going to bring her in?"

"It wouldn't do any good. People like Alicia would rather die than talk. But at least now we know, we can keep her under surveillance. I have people on that now."

"Anything else of interest in there?"

"The most interesting thing was what *wasn't* in there."

"How do you mean?"

"Well, considering the file had your name on it, there was no mention of you in any of the papers. But then, my people believe that some papers have been removed."

"What do you think that means?"

"I have no idea, but we did get a few other names though, and they're now under surveillance."

"So are we any closer to TDO?" I asked.

"Right now? No, but I'm hopeful the surveillance on the names we uncovered might turn up something."

"What are you and Blaze working on at the moment?"

"Don't mention that useless lump to me."

Whoops. I'd obviously said the wrong thing. Blaze was Daze's little sidekick—a kind of apprentice Rogue Retriever.

"What's he done?"

"Fallen asleep, that's what he's done. When he should have been watching a werewolf who's been killing humans. We'd had him under surveillance for some time, but he got away—so we're back to square one."

"You're not having a good day then?"

"I'm not having a good month. Apart from that useless article, I've got the 'UO's' to put up with."

"UO's?"

"Unlicensed Operators. There's only a small number of licensed Rogue Retrievers, but there's an ever growing army of amateurs who think they can make a quick buck by going after Rogues. They cause all kinds of problems. I don't much care if they put their own lives in jeopardy, but they're a danger to others—sups and humans alike." She took a deep breath. "Anyway, you don't want to listen to all of my problems. What's new with you?"

"Just the usual stuff. I'm currently negotiating a publishing deal for my cat."

Chapter 10

I hadn't been expecting Dot Comm, but she was waiting for me at the office. Mrs V had given her a scarf, and was trying to persuade her to take a pair of socks when I arrived.

"I don't really need this." Dot held out the scarf once we were in my office.

"Take it with you would you? Mrs V gets upset if people reject her scarves. There's a charity shop just around the corner. You could drop it off there on your way out. Last time I checked, they'd got quite a few of Mrs V's creations in there."

Dot nodded, and put the scarf in her bag. "I've come to tell you to drop the case, and to let me have your bill."

"Oh? I heard they were exhuming the body. What happened?"

"Ron wasn't happy about it, but I'm glad they did it. The body was Reg's, so that means the police were barking up the wrong tree. Ron is in the clear."

"Right. Well I guess there's nothing more for me to do. I'll get Mrs V to post the bill on to you."

My father had always insisted that you should only work on a case if someone was paying you. He was right—I knew that. But in a case like this, it was hard to let it go. Despite my father's words ringing in my ears, I was determined to get to the bottom of Gina Peel's murder. What did it matter if I wasn't being paid, anyway? I'd soon be raking it in with my ten per cent cut from Winky's bestselling book.

It seemed it was a day for unexpected visitors. Colonel

Briggs showed up not long after Dot Comm had left. He was carrying an enormous wooden box with what appeared to be jokers painted on each side.

"Do you need a hand?" I offered.

"It's okay. Do you mind if I put it down over there?" He pointed to the sofa. "It's heavier than it looks."

"Of course."

It took him a few seconds to catch his breath. "What do you think to it?"

"Err — it's very nice. What is it?"

"A jack-in-the-box of course." He slipped open the catch.

"No!" I screamed." I'd always been terrified of jack-in-the-boxes.

Too late — I closed my eyes.

"Are you okay, Jill?" The colonel sounded concerned.

I opened my eyes, and realised that the jack was still firmly in the box.

"Yes. I was just — err — I thought Winky was going to jump on the desk."

Out of the corner of my eye, I could see Winky giving me a puzzled look.

"It needs a little work." The colonel closed the lid.

"Is it a present for someone?"

"Yes, for myself." He laughed. "Didn't I mention that I collect antique and unusual toys?"

"I don't think so."

"I really must show you my 'toy room' some time."

"Do you have any clowns in there?"

"Clowns? No, I don't think so. Why?"

"No reason."

"Tinker is looking well," he said. 'Tinker' was the colonel's name for Winky.

Winky hissed at him. He wasn't a fan of the colonel's—probably because he could smell the scents of a thousand dogs on him.

"How's that Mutt of yours doing?"

"Barry? He's okay. Got his eye on a young lady dog at the moment."

"I trust you've had him snipped?"

"It's in my diary."

"Hope you didn't mind me dropping in unannounced. I was in town and wanted to ask if you'd like to help with our latest charity push."

"Sure." I grabbed my handbag and was about to get out my purse.

"I'm not here for your cash. We're having a sponsored event, and I thought you might like to take part."

"I'm not a great one for walks, if I'm honest."

"That's okay. No walking involved."

"Maybe then. What does it entail?"

"Well, I know your job takes you into a few sticky situations, so when we decided on skydiving, I thought you'd be keen to have a go."

"Skydiving?"

"Exciting, eh. Just a pity I'm too old."

"Diving? Out of a plane?"

"You'll be strapped to an experienced skydiver, obviously."

Obviously.

"So, what do you say? Can I put your name down?"

I shook my head. "Sorry."

"I thought this would be right up your street."

Jumping out of a plane with nothing between me and the ground—sounds great.

"Sorry, Colonel. I have a fear — "

"Of flying? Of heights?"

"Of dying."

"Peter has signed up."

"He has?" I'd thought he was insane when he married Kathy — now I had proof.

"Are you sure I can't persuade you?"

"Sorry, Colonel. It's not for me. I'll sponsor Peter obviously."

"And you'll come to the big day?"

"To see Peter jump out of a plane? I wouldn't miss it for the world."

Winky came out from under the sofa as soon as the colonel had left.

"Can I do it?" he said.

"What?"

"The skydive. Sounds like a lot of fun."

"Your idea of fun and mine are very different."

"So, can I do it?"

"I'll ask the colonel the first chance I get."

"Promise?"

"Would I lie?"

I rang Kathy.

"How much have you got Peter insured for?"

"Sorry?"

"Have you taken out life insurance on Peter?"

"What are you going on about, Jill? Is this your latest plan to try to bolster your meagre earnings, by selling insurance on the side?"

"No. I'll have you know I've billed a client earlier today."

"How many bills have you sent out this month?"

"I forget."

"Double figures?"

"Not quite."

"More than five?"

"Close."

"How close? Is it closer to five or zero?"

"Zero."

"Is that the only bill you've issued?"

"Yes, but never mind that. Why are you letting Peter skydive?"

"Why not? It'll be fun. He's looking forward to it."

"You two are both insane. You do know what skydiving is, don't you? There's no water involved."

"It's perfectly safe. He'll be attached to a qualified instructor."

"How does that make it safer? It's twice the weight falling to the ground."

"Pete said the colonel was going to ask you to take part."

"He just did."

"What did you say to him? *'No, thanks. I'm a coward'.*"

"I'm not a coward."

"So you're going to do it?"

"I have to be brave in my line of work."

"So, *you are* going to do it then?"

"Fearless even."

"You're not doing it, are you?"

"Of course not. Do you think I'm insane?"

***

The Gina Peel murder was an itch I couldn't scratch. I wasn't exactly overrun with work, so what harm could a little more sniffing around do? I turned to my trusty friend — the Bugle, and reread some of the articles on the murder of Gina Peel. One thing I'd missed the first time around was a quote from a friend of hers — one Julie Truman. It wasn't difficult to track down her number, so I gave her a call on the off-chance.

"Thanks for seeing me so quickly." It was only two hours since I'd called her, and I was now in her apartment. She had exquisite taste — a sixties theme — just like my place. "I love your apartment."

"You do? I recently moved in and the furniture came with it. It's ghastly. I'm waiting for someone to come and take it to the dump, so I can get some modern stuff in. Who'd want this kind of thing in their home?"

Obviously I'd been wrong. The woman had no taste. Still, that wasn't why I was there.

"I was hired by Dorothy Comm to look into the murder of Ron Peel."

"Dot? We've met a few times. Strange name."

"I suppose so. I hadn't thought about it. What can you tell me about Gina?"

"She and I had been friends ever since university. One of her brothers died in a climbing accident not long after uni. I remember her being very upset at the time."

"Did you know either of her brothers?"

"I never actually met the one who died. I've met Ron two or three times, but I wouldn't say I know him well. I got the impression that Gina had been closer to her other brother — what was his name?"

"Reg."

"Oh yeah. How could I have forgotten that?"

"Had you seen her recently?"

"We had coffee the week before she was murdered. And I spoke to her on the phone the day it happened."

"Did she seem okay?"

"She wasn't happy. There'd been a water leak at her place which had got into the electrics. She'd had to move out. I offered to put her up, but she said she'd already found somewhere to stay."

"Did she tell you where?"

"Yes, she gave me the address. It's where they found her body."

"Did she say how she'd found the apartment, or who it belonged to?"

"No, and at the time it didn't seem important."

***

I was strangely excited at the prospect of my date. Love Spell had arranged for me to meet my 'match' at Kaleidoscope which was one of the restaurants they used for first dates. I'd never been there before, but it had a reputation for good food. It was only now I began to think about the business model Love Spell operated. It was strange to say the least. Any witch who found her partner though the service was committed to keep a major secret from him for the rest of their lives together. Curiously, it would have been easier for me than for most witches. After all, I had lived among humans — totally oblivious to the fact that I was a witch — for most of my life. For a witch who'd lived all of her life in Candlefield, it would be very difficult to adjust.

My date's name was Ryan Day. I'd seen a photo of him,

and he was certainly a looker. In the back of my mind I was always a little suspicious of good looking guys who felt the need to sign up for dating web sites or agencies. Hilary had told me it wasn't that unusual, and often it was a question of time constraints. Everyone was so busy these days they didn't have time to seek out a partner by a more conventional route.

I arrived ten minutes early, so I got a drink and waited by the bar. It was really quiet, and the barman, Scott, was quite chatty.

"Waiting for someone?" He flashed me a smile. This guy would definitely not need the services of a dating agency.

"Yeah. We have a table booked." I hoped the 'we' might keep him at bay.

"You'll enjoy it. The food is excellent. Have you been here before?"

"No. First time."

"You timed it right. We had a major revamp when the new owner took over six months ago. There's a new chef too — he's won several awards."

Before I could respond, a voice from behind me drew my attention.

"Jill?"

I recognised Ryan's face from his photo. He was just as good looking in real life.

The barman had been right. The food was top notch. The company was excellent too. Ryan, who worked in sports management, was charming, interesting and funny. Everything I look for in a man. Wouldn't it be ironic if this date ended in a relationship?

"I've really enjoyed tonight," Ryan said as we made our way out. "Could I see you again?"

"That would be nice." Who needs Luther?

We didn't exchange phone numbers because we were meant to make arrangements via the dating agency for the first two dates.

"Great, I'll call the agency to arrange it," he said, after walking me to my car.

From a personal point of view, the date had gone really well. From a professional point of view, I'd learned nothing of any value. Our liaison had gone without a hitch, and would no doubt be counted as a success in the Love Spell statistics.

Chapter 11

I woke up the next morning, full of the joys of spring. My date with Ryan had gone really well, and although it was meant to be a work assignment I was optimistic it might develop into more than that. What? Who are you calling a floozy? Look, I know it might look as though I had four men on the go, but let's be honest. Luther and I were dead in the water. Jack blew hot and cold. Drake had issues he needed to deal with. That left the path clear for Ryan — the love of my life.

There was a frantic pounding at the door of my flat. Maybe Luther had seen the error of his ways, and wanted to try again with me?
I should be so lucky.
"Mr Ivers?" Mr Ivers was my boring neighbour.
"Jill, you have to help me!"
I'd never seen him look so distressed. Or so wet. He looked as though he'd climbed out of a swimming pool — fully dressed.
"What happened?"
"There's been some kind of water leak in my flat. Everything is soaked."
What was it with the water leaks? Gina Peel had moved out because of one, and now poor old Mr Ivers seemed to have a plumbing problem.
"Have you turned the water off?"
"I don't know how. All of my movie journals have been ruined. What will I do? They're irreplaceable."
Every burst pipe has a silver lining. What? Don't pretend you hadn't thought the same thing.

"You go and find the maintenance guy. He's usually in that little office in the basement. I'll go see what I can salvage in your flat. Is the door unlocked?"

"Yes."

"Okay then. Get going."

Poor Mr Ivers. He hadn't been kidding about the water. Everything was soaked. There wasn't much I could do about the furniture, but maybe I could help with the only things he really cared about. I found his journals on the table in the kitchen. Who knew he had so many? I carried the sodden books out into the corridor, and laid them side by side. There were fifteen in total. I could hear footsteps in the distance, so I knew I wouldn't have much time. I cast the 'take it back' spell — one of the first spells I ever learned.

The maintenance man, Charlie Marley, appeared with Mr Ivers in tow.

"Make way!" He hurried past me into the flat.

Mr Ivers stared at the journals with wide eyes. "How?"

I managed to get them out before they got too wet." I lied.

"But they were saturated. I saw them. They were ruined."

"Doesn't look like it does it?" I opened up the one closest to me. "See, dry as a bone. You must have panicked."

His expression was a curious blend of confusion and delight.

"Oh, Jill — I don't know how I'll ever be able to thank you."

You could start by never talking to me ever again. What? It's not like I actually said it out loud.

***

Before I went into the office, I decided to make a call to Love Spell. I was keen to report back, but even more keen to arrange a second date with Ryan.

"Is that Hilary?"

"No, it's Milly."

"It's Jill Gooder."

"Morning, Jill."

"I'm calling about my date with Ryan."

"Actually I just came off the phone with him."

Wow! He was even keener than I was. This was a very good sign.

"Did he say when he wanted to meet up again?"

"Actually, he said he didn't."

"Didn't what?"

"Want to meet up with you again. He said you weren't a match."

"Are you sure? I thought the date went well."

"Not from his point of view. He actually said—err—it doesn't matter."

"Go on. Tell me."

"He said it was the worst date he'd ever had."

I was so stunned I ended the call right there. How had I got it so wrong? I thought we'd really hit it off. He hadn't done or said anything to make me think we weren't compatible. Was I really so delusional? Ten minutes later, when I'd composed myself, I called back.

"Milly, it's Jill again. Sorry about that. I had to take another call. Look, I have to say I'm surprised by Ryan's reaction. I thought the evening had gone well. Anyway, it does make me wonder if there might be something untoward going on. I'll stay on it and let you know if I find anything."

***

"You have to do something about that noise," Mrs V said, as soon as I arrived at the office.

"What is it?" It sounded like some kind of machine, and it was coming from next door.

"I've no idea. It started about twenty minutes ago. I can hardly hear myself think. How am I meant to write my book or knit?"

"Or do any work?"

"Exactly. It's impossible. You'll have to go around there and talk to them."

"I will, but there's something I need to attend to in my office first."

"You mean that stupid cat."

"If I don't feed him, my life won't be worth living."

"Please hurry up. I can feel one of my migraines coming on."

Once inside my office, I started towards the cupboard where I kept the cat food.

"Never mind about that!" Winky screamed at me.

This had to be some kind of weird dream. That could be the only explanation for Winky telling me not to bother with his food.

"You have to do something about that noise. How am I supposed to finish off 'Bruce' with all that racket going on?"

This was probably the first time Mrs V and Winky had ever seen eye to eye. In Winky's case, just the one eye obviously.

"How am I meant to write," he said while holding his

head. "Your five per cent is at stake here."

"It's ten."

"What is?"

"My cut. We agreed ten."

"Are you sure?"

I pulled out the pocket recorder and hit play: *'Ten or I get the old bag lady to do it. Okay, ten it is'*.

I'm no mug. I left nothing to chance where Winky was concerned.

He shrugged. "Must have slipped my mind. All the more reason to go round there and put a stop to that noise."

The noise was coming from an office in the same building as ours. It had previously belonged to a company which specialised in the importation of pogo sticks. They'd been bounced out of there by Gordon Armitage to make way for his law empire. I knocked on the door. There was no reply. I wasn't sure if that meant there was no one home or if they simply hadn't heard me because of the infernal noise coming from inside. After two more attempts, I tried the door — it was open.

Inside the room was a giant machine which looked like an industrial printing press. Standing next to it was a young woman wearing huge ear defenders. She was singing something, but I couldn't make out what.

"Hello!" I yelled at the top of my voice.

No response.

"Hi, there!"

Still nothing.

I walked over to the machine. Once I was standing in her line of sight, I waved my hands around.

"Hi." She mouthed the word.

"Can you switch this thing off?" I yelled.

She made a gesture which indicated I should wait. Moments later, she hit a big red button and the machine ground slowly to a halt.

"Sorry, I couldn't hear you," the young woman said. She'd taken off the ear defenders which were now looped around her neck. "What did you say?"

"I asked you to turn this off."

She smiled. "Oh, right. Sorry."

"I'm Jill Gooder. I have the office next door. We can't hear ourselves think in there."

"I'm not surprised. I told him this was a stupid place to put Bertha."

"Who's Bertha?"

"That's what I call this old gal."

"Who decided to put it here?" As if I didn't know.

"Mr Armitage."

"Gordon?"

"I'm not sure. I never know which one of them is which."

"Handkerchief in his breast pocket?"

"Yeah that's the guy," she said. "I don't trust a man with a handkerchief in his pocket."

"Really? Me neither. Why did he insist on putting Bertha here?"

"No idea. It took an army of men to move her here over the weekend. We used to be in the basement which was a much better spot. Look, I'm sorry about the noise, but there's not much I can do about it. I don't like it up here, but I'm the only person in the office who knows how to use this monster."

"That's okay. I'll take it up with your bosses."

I'd had an idea.

I went outside, and made my way around to the alleyway which ran between my building and the one behind it. I knew which window I needed, but there was no convenient fire escape to get me up there. Grandma's words came back to my mind — 'it's all about spell selection'. The roads at either end of the alleyway were busy, and the alley itself was a popular thoroughfare. I didn't have the luxury of time, so I'd have to resort to the 'jump' spell.

First, I put in a call to Mrs V, and told her that I needed her to get the operator out of the room just long enough for me to get in and 'work my magic'.

I made the call.

"Mrs V?"

"Hello?"

I'd forgotten to take into account that Mrs V was a bit deaf at the best of times, and even more so now she had the noise of the printing press to contend with.

"Mrs V! Can you hear me?"

"No need to shout, dear."

Give me strength.

It took me a while, but in the end I brought her up to speed.

"I need you to get around there now!" I shouted.

"Do you want me to go next door now?"

"Yes!"

"Pardon?"

"Yes!"

"I'm on my way."

I checked the alleyway — it was clear. I'd only have one chance to get this right.

I cast the 'jump' spell and leapt towards the building behind mine. I judged it just right. From there I bounced back and forth until I landed on the window ledge outside the room with the printing press in it. The glass in the window was frosted, but I could see a shape moving around inside. Moments later, the shape disappeared. Mrs V had done her part—now I had to do mine. The window was partially open—presumably because of the large amount of heat generated by the machine. I pulled it open and climbed inside. I could see two figures out on the landing. Mrs V was no doubt confusing the operator with some story or other. I unplugged the machine, cast the 'power' spell and then lifted it, and carried it to the opposite wall. Then I cast the 'invisible' spell and made myself disappear—just in the nick of time.

The operator stared at the wall where the machine had once been, and then at the machine which was now on the opposite wall. Then for several moments, she glanced back and forth between the two—desperately trying to work out what had happened.

Still looking confused, she picked up the landline, and made a call.

"Mr Armitage. It's Belinda. Yes, that's right: 'the printing woman'. There's something funny going on up here. The machine has moved. Of course I'm sure. No, I haven't had a drink. Can you come and take a look please?"

All the time she was talking, she had her back to me. I took the opportunity to pick the machine up again and move it to the outer wall. When she ended her call and turned around, she looked horrified.

"What's all this about?" Armitage said when he burst through the door.

"It's moved again," she said without taking her eyes off the printing press.

It was Armitage's turn to look confused.

"It was over there." He pointed to the first wall. "Did you move it?"

"How could I have moved it? It was there, and then there and now here."

"The machine can't have moved itself."

"It just did."

"Well, never mind. It's perfectly all right there."

"I'm not working in here." The operator started for the door. "This room is haunted."

"You can't leave."

"Watch me."

"But—you're the only one who knows how to operate this beast."

"Tough. I'm off down the job centre."

"Wait! I'll have it moved back to the basement."

"I'm not using it until you do."

"I'll get it done tonight."

Yes! Result!

Chapter 12

Mrs V was all smiles when I got back to the office.

"How did you manage that?" she asked.

"I asked Gordon Armitage nicely."

"I know that's not true. That horrible man would never do anything just because you asked him to. Whatever you did, thank you."

Winky was hard at work on his manuscript—no word of thanks from him, but what had I expected?

"You might be getting a call later from a Wayne Starr," he said, without looking up.

"Another publisher?"

"Nah. This guy wants to talk movie rights."

"I don't know anything about negotiating movie deals."

"You don't know anything about being a P.I., but you always seem to bluff your way through."

Cheek of the cat.

"Same fifteen per cent cut?" I said.

"It's ten."

"Oh, yeah. Of course."

It was worth a try.

An hour later, when Winky had decided to take a nap and allow me access to my computer, I was going over the Peel murder and the Love Spell cases.

Just then, the door to my office flew open.

"You can't go in there!" Mrs V shouted.

"Just watch me." Alicia slammed the door closed behind her.

"Nice of you to drop in," I said.

"Cut the smartass, Gooder."

"I take it this is not a social call. On your way to do some lawyering?"

"See. That's what I mean. You just can't control that mouth of yours can you?"

Winky was awake now, and he began to hiss at the intruder.

"What is that thing?" Alicia pulled a face. "What did you do to its eye?"

Winky hissed even louder.

"That's Winky. He knows a rat when he smells one."

"I've tried the nice approach with you," she said. "Now I'm warning you. Call off your minions."

The nice approach presumably being the time she poisoned me.

"I have no idea what you are talking about."

"I'm not an idiot. I know what you and Daisy Flowers are up to."

Alicia was either braver than I'd thought or way stupider. Calling Daze by her real name was not a good idea.

"Those idiots you have tailing me couldn't be more obvious if they were wearing clown paint and big clown shoes."

"Is that all you came here to say?"

"No. I thought it only fair to warn you that if you insist on pursuing this pointless investigation then there'll be consequences."

"Is that a threat?" I laughed. "Bring it on. Do your worst."

I really should learn to keep my big mouth shut.

"Your actions may have dire consequences for others."

"Others? What others?"

"I believe you know Raven."

"Where is he? What have you done to him?"

"He's okay." She glared at me for the longest moment. "For now at least."

"If you lay a hand on him—"

"You'll what? Don't make threats you can't back up. Do you honestly think you'd be a match for those with real powers?"

"Who are 'those' exactly? What do you know about TDO?"

"I've said what I came here to say. Just be careful—I'd hate to see you get hurt." Her smile was even scarier than her angry face.

"Well thank you for calling. If you ask Mrs V politely on the way out, I'm sure she'll set you up with a nice scarf."

"Who was that horrible person?" Mrs V asked after Alicia had left.

"Just someone I had coffee with once."

"What did you do to upset her? She was ghastly—a right little witch."

I wasn't sure if I should let Drake know what Alicia had said, but in the end decided it would serve no purpose, and would cause him even more worry. Instead I called Daze who was busy in the latest of her 'cover' jobs—dog walker.

"I can barely hear you," I said.

"Sorry, Jill. I have you on earphones. I need both hands to keep hold of this lot."

"How many dogs are you walking?"

"Seven. It should have been eight, but the Shih Tzu had the runs. It's not as if I even like dogs. What did Alicia have to say?"

I brought Daze up to speed as best I could—given all the barking.

"I'm not happy that she spotted her shadows so easily," Daze said. "I'll have to kick someone's ass. I'll see about getting some new people assigned to her. I might even pull Blaze off what he's doing and get him onto it."

"What happened to the werewolf you were trailing? It was a full moon last night wasn't it?"

"Total disaster. He gave us the slip—again. Goodness knows what havoc he might have caused last night—I'm still waiting for the reports to come in. Stop that!" She shouted at the dogs. "Sorry, Jill, I'll have to go—we're almost at the park. I'll never be able to keep hold of them, and talk to you, once we're in there."

"Okay."

"One last thing though, Jill. You really need to find Raven. I fear for his safety."

"I'll do my best. Bye."

***

After my encounter with Alicia I needed to get out of the office for a while. Not that anyone would notice my absence. Mrs V and Winky were both too engrossed in their respective literary endeavours.

I'd really enjoyed the coffee I had at The Coffee Triangle, so thought I'd pay it another visit. On the back of the loyalty card, instead of pictures of coffee cups, there were little images of the instruments—a nice touch, I thought.

It hadn't taken long for someone to take over the premises which had, until recently, been Rod's Rods. There were two builders' vans parked on the pavement outside, and scaffolding covering the front of the building. I pressed my nose against the window to try and see what was going on inside.

"Nosey, aren't you?" Grandma appeared at the door of the shop. She was wearing a yellow hard hat.

"Nice hat."

She gave me 'that' look.

"Is this your place now?" I said.

"We're going to knock through from Ever A Wool Moment."

"Business must be booming."

"It is, but that's not the reason for the expansion. I'm going to open a small tea room, so the punters can have a drink while they chat and knit."

"It was very fortunate that the shop next door became vacant."

"It was, wasn't it? The poor man seemed to have a run of bad luck."

She'd been responsible—I was sure of it. The flood, rats and power cuts—it had to have been her doing.

"Anyway," she said. "Apart from sticking your nose into my business, what are you doing? Haven't you got any cases you should be working on?"

"As it happens, I'm working on two cases right now. I was on my way to that new coffee shop around the corner. Have you seen it?"

"I haven't seen it, but I've heard it. Damn row with their stupid drums and gongs."

"I quite like it."

"You would."

What was that supposed to mean? I didn't get the chance

to ask because she disappeared back inside the shop. Grandma's empire was expanding. Not satisfied with ruling the world of yarn, she was now moving into the tea room business. I just hoped she didn't decide to open shop in Candlefield. Cuppy C wouldn't stand a chance against her marketing machine.

***

I felt much better after a latte and ten minutes banging on a drum. I'd been a little disappointed only to get a snare drum, but the tenor and bass drums had already been snagged.

In between writing chapters of her book, I'd had Mrs V track down the name of the maintenance company who looked after the apartment block where Gina Peel used to live. The man who'd been called out to the leak in her apartment was apparently called Joe. He covered a number of buildings in the Washbridge area, so we'd arranged to meet in the car park outside of Ultimate Plumbing Supplies—a superstore for the plumbing trade. I spotted his van which had the word 'WIMPS' in large letters on the side. Only when I got closer did I see the full name: Washbridge Industrial Maintenance and Plumbing Services.

I pulled up alongside and gave him a wave. He smiled, climbed out of the van, and came over to my car.

"Jill Gooder?" He had an accent which I couldn't place.

"Hi." I climbed out of the car and shook his hand. "Thanks for agreeing to talk to me."

"No problem. Rather be talking to a pretty lady than have

my head stuck under an 'S' bend."

I smiled. It was reassuring to know that I compared favourably to the underside of a sink. Joe was middle-aged with a beer belly, but he had a certain charm.

"Yeah, I remember that job." He said while rubbing his stubbly chin. "Mind you, I probably wouldn't have remembered it if it hadn't been for that woman being murdered. Nasty job that. Is that what you're investigating?"

"Yes. I understand the water got into the electrics, so she was forced to move out."

"That's right. It wasn't a big job. One of the pipes from the tank had come loose. Only took me a few minutes to sort out."

"Did you notice anything unusual?"

"Not really."

"You don't sound sure."

"Well to be honest, I've never seen one of those pipes come loose like that. Once they're fixed in place, they usually stay there."

"Could it have been loosened deliberately?"

"It's possible, but I couldn't say for sure."

"Has anyone else talked to you about this?"

"What? Like the police you mean? No. You're the only one."

I thanked Joe, and he drove away in his WIMPS van. I couldn't help but think he must have got some stick from his friends over that acronym.

I knew fate could be a strange thing, but I'd always been bothered by the fact that Gina Peel was killed in an apartment that she'd only moved to temporarily because of a water leak. Now Joe had suggested that the leak might have been caused deliberately, I was even more intrigued. I had to find out more about the apartment where she died.

***

Normally I'd go out of my way to avoid Betty Longbottom—there was only so much sea shell news I could stand. But the poor woman was obviously struggling as she hobbled along the corridor in front of me.

"Are you okay, Betty?"

She turned to face me. The grimace on her face answered my question.

"Hi, Jill."

"Are you alright?"

"Yeah." She managed a smile. "It's nothing. My own silly fault really."

"What happened?"

"Norman and I had a day at the seaside."

"Looking for shells?"

"Yes, and bottle tops."

"Of course."

"Anyway, I insisted on paddling through the rock pools. Norman told me he'd seen a few large crabs around, but—well."

"You got bitten?"

"Not bitten—pincered. It was enormous, and it had a hold of my big toe."

"Ouch." Just the thought of it brought tears to my eyes.

"What happened? Did Norman pull it off?"

"He wanted to, but he's allergic to crustaceans. They bring

him out in a rash."

"Nasty."

"I managed to shake it off eventually, but not before it had made a real mess of my toe. It's all red and swollen, and the nail has turned blue. Would you like to see it?" She started to take off her shoe.

"No!" I yelled a little too loudly. "It's okay. Where is Norman?"

"He's at his place. The shock brought on his bad stomach, so he's staying in bed for a while."

"Poor you. Well I'd better get going. I hope your toe gets better soon."

Back inside my flat, I decided to scrap my original plan to go out for a sea-food platter.

Chapter 13

"So how did the date go?" Kathy asked when I called around at her place. For a moment the question threw me. I couldn't think how she would have known about the date which Love Spell had arranged. Then the penny dropped, and I realised she meant my meal at Jack Maxwell's place.

"It was okay."

"That good, eh?"

"No, it was nice."

"Nice? Steady my beating heart."

"What do you want me to say? It was a nice evening. The meal was delicious—"

"So, Jack can cook then?"

"No. He brought in a chef."

Kathy laughed.

"He tried to make out he'd made it all himself, but then I went into the kitchen and saw Gordon Blare."

"Who's he?"

"The same chef I used when Luther came around."

She laughed. "Oh yes. Tell me again how the date with Luther went. I want to hear the full *account*."

"You're not funny."

"I'm sorry. I didn't mean to rub it in, but I really thought Luther was a keeper." She hesitated, and I knew what was coming. "A *bookkeeper*." She was bent double, laughing.

"I don't think it's funny."

Kathy reached for a tissue and began to dab at her eyes.

"I'm sorry. The whole thing must have been really *taxing* for you."

"Have you been saving these up?"

She was still trying to get her breath when Peter appeared. "Is she giving you a hard time?" he said.

"Doesn't she always?"

"Anyway, I have a bone to pick with you," he said.

"What have I done now?"

"Do you remember what you told Kathy about the conmen?"

"Yeah. Mrs V told me to warn you they were targeting anglers."

"Were they her exact words?"

"I don't remember exactly. Why?"

"I walked all around the lake telling all the other anglers. It took me ages, but then when I got to one of the last guys, he just laughed at me. It turned out he's something of a computer nerd. The con men aren't going after anglers. It has nothing to do with 'fishing'. It's 'phishing' with a PH."

"What's that?"

"I'm not sure. He tried to explain it, but it was all nonsense to me. Something about emails and web pages that pretend to be something they aren't."

"Why's it called phishing?"

He shrugged. "Anyway, thanks for making me look like an idiot. The guys took the mickey out of me in the pub all night for that one."

The kids were out at their friends' houses. Lizzie was at Kylie's, and Mikey was at Jimmy's. Peter made dinner for us — roast chicken, mash and Yorkshire pudding with an assortment of vegetables. And he did it without the help of Gordon Blare.

"You look tired, Peter," I said. "Is the colonel overworking you?"

He shook his head. "No. Work is fine. We just didn't get much sleep last night, did we Kathy?"

"None of us did," she said. "I told you about the new neighbour, didn't I?"

"Is he still making a lot of noise?"

"Last night was the worst yet. It was one in the morning before we finally got any sleep."

"I wanted to go around and have a word," Peter said. "But Kathy said I should leave it. Something has to be done though—it's getting ridiculous."

The meal was great, and I enjoyed the chance to chat with the two of them without the kids running riot. I left at the same time as Peter set off to collect them. Much as I loved my nephew and niece, I was shattered and couldn't face the mayhem.

As I drove home, I thought about what Kathy and Peter had said about their new neighbour, and then I remembered that the previous night had been a full moon.

I had a voicemail from Drake. He wanted to talk, and suggested we meet in the park the following day. He said he'd be there at ten o'clock in the morning, and I only need call him back if I couldn't make it. I'd planned to go over to Candlefield anyway, and it was time I had a chat with him about Raven.

***

There was no sign of Betty when I got back to my flat, but I did walk straight into Mr Ivers. He beamed when he caught sight of me — I was no doubt a hero in his eyes for rescuing the movie journals. He'd probably still be thanking me for the next five years.

"Jill, I'm glad I caught you. There's something I have to say to you —"

"It's okay, Mr Ivers. There really is no need for thanks. Anyone would have done it."

"No, but —"

"I'd rather we just forgot about it. Your journals are safe and that's all that matters."

"That's not why I wanted a word."

"Oh?"

"You saw the damage to my flat."

"I did. It was a terrible thing."

"It's going to cost me a fortune to put right."

"Still, the insurance should cover it."

"That'll cover part of the cost, thank goodness, but not all of it. That's why I wanted to talk to you."

I didn't believe it. He was going to try to tap me for a loan. Well he was out of luck. I was barely making rent myself.

"I'm sorry to tell you I'll have to increase the cost of the newsletter subscription."

"The newsletter?"

"Yes, and I'm afraid it's going to be quite an increase. Double in fact."

"That's a lot."

"But worth every penny, I'm sure you'll agree. When I thought the journals were lost, I seriously considered packing it in altogether."

"Hold on. Are you saying if I hadn't rescued those journals, you'd have given the newsletter up?"

"Precisely."

Hoisted by my own petard.

"Look Mr Ivers. I'm really sorry about what happened to your flat, but I can't afford to pay double. I think I'm going to have to cancel."

"Are you sure?"

I sighed, and tried to look suitably disappointed. "I think so."

"Even with the cancellation fee?"

"What cancellation fee?"

"Don't you remember the paper you signed?"

"I thought that was just the Direct Debit agreement."

"Didn't you read the small print on the back?"

The small print? "What did it say?"

"It specified that you'll have to pay the equivalent of two years' cover price to cancel."

"Let me see if I've got this right. I can keep on getting the newsletter, or pay for two years to cancel?"

"That's about the size of it. I'll leave you to mull it over."

Curiously, the option to cancel still seemed the more appealing of the two.

***

I was in Candlefield bright and early the next day. The sky was blue, the sun was out and Barry was being more like Barry.

"Can we go for a walk?"

"Yes. That's where we're going now."

"I love to walk!"

"Yes. I know you do."

"Are we going for a walk?"

"Yes."

"When?"

"Right now."

"Great. Let's go!"

"You seem much happier than the last time I saw you," I said.

"That nice vet gave me lots of treats."

"The vet? Have you been poorly?"

"No. I had the snap. It wasn't too bad. I was asleep while he did it."

"Who took you to the vet?"

"Lucy."

I was surprised, but kind of relieved. I was a bit squeamish when it came to that kind of thing.

I knocked on the window of Cuppy C, and caught Amber's attention.

"Going to the park!" I mouthed.

She gave me the thumbs up.

I glanced across the road, and saw the cakes in Best Cakes were now earthbound. Aunt Lucy must have relented and reversed the spell. Presumably, not before Miles had promised to say nothing to the twins.

Drake was already waiting for me in the park. It seemed an age since I'd seen him. Our two dogs were soon chasing one another around, which left us free to talk.

"Have you heard from Raven?" I asked.

He shook his head. Should I tell him about the threats which Alicia had made against his brother? I decided against it — no point in worrying him unduly.

"I have discovered something though," he said. "I tracked down one of his friends, and according to him, Raven has been hanging around with a gang for the last year or so."

"What kind of gang?"

"I don't know. The only information I could get out of him was the name: The Skulls."

"Nice. And you have no idea where they hang out?"

He shook his head.

"I'll see what I can find out."

"Thanks, Jill. I really do appreciate your help."

It was the least I could do after misjudging Drake so badly.

"I'd really like for us to go out together sometime—unless you're seeing someone?" he said.

Was I seeing someone? Luther Stone—only in my dreams. Jack Maxwell—maybe, but who knew?

"I'd like that."

"Maybe you could come around to my place," he said. "I could cook us a meal. I'm quite the cook, even if I do say so myself."

Yeah—I'd heard that one before.

"I think I'd like to eat out if it's all the same to you."

"Sure. No problem. In Candlefield or in Washbridge?"

"In Candlefield, I think. You pick somewhere and let me know. I'm sure we'll be able to find a night when we're both free."

I made the mistake of telling Barry it was time for us to go home before I had him on the lead. I could see Drake laughing in the distance, as he walked his well behaved dog to the gates. I was left chasing Barry up and down the park. By the time I eventually cornered him, I was absolutely exhausted.

"That was fun!" Barry said.

"Are you okay, Jill?" Pearl said. I'd taken Barry upstairs, and then gone back down to the tea room. "You look kind of —"

"Shattered? I am. I've just spent the last fifteen minutes chasing that soft dog all around the park."

"You should have taken the 'Barkies' with you."

"What are 'Barkies'?"

"They're a dog treat. They're brilliant. It's what the vet gave Barry after he'd had the snip. He goes wild for them, so whenever we take him for a walk, we put a handful in our pockets. When we want him to come to us, all we have to do is shout, 'Barkies'."

"Don't people give you funny looks?"

"Sometimes, but it's worth it."

"I wish you'd told me about them before I took him out today."

"Amber said *she* was going to tell you."

"No, I didn't." Amber had walked through from the cake counter. "You said *you'd* tell her."

"Did not!"

"Did too!"

"Okay, okay." I stepped in. "At least I know about them now. Sounds like they're worth their weight in gold. I'll have a cup of coffee, and then I'll get back to Washbridge."

"You can't go back," Amber said.

"Have you forgotten?" Pearl pointed to the notice board.

"Is that today?"

The fancy dress competition had completely slipped my mind.

"Sorry girls. I don't think I can make it."

"You have to, Jill."

"Yeah, you promised."

Synchronised pouting — got to love it.

"Did you two get costumes?"

"We did."

"Salt and pepper?"

"No chance. That was a stupid idea — even by Mum's standards."

"So what did you get? Show me."

"You have to wait until tonight. It's a surprise."

"Have you seen each other's costumes?"

They both nodded. That was a relief; they had a bad habit of buying identical outfits.

"Okay. I guess I can stay. I hope I'm not the only one there without a costume though."

"You won't be."

"Do you know someone else who is going without a costume?"

"No, that's not what we meant."

They giggled. It was never a good sign when they giggled. "What?"

They giggled some more and then the light bulb went on.

"You didn't. Tell me you didn't!"

"We did. We couldn't let you go without a costume."

"What is it?"

"We can't tell you — it's a secret. You'll find out tonight. You're going to love it."

Somehow, I doubted that.

Chapter 14

"No way!" I protested. "Not happening!"

"Come on, Jill," Pearl said, only just managing to keep a straight face. "It took us ages to find it."

"Yeah, come on, Jill," Amber said. "Don't be a spoilsport."

"How come you get to dress up as a mermaid, and Pearl gets to dress up as a princess, but I have to dress up as a custard cream?"

"You love custard creams."

"I love to eat them. That doesn't mean I want to walk down the street dressed as one."

"If that's what you're worried about, it's okay. Alan will give you a lift to the hall."

"I like your costume." Grandma cackled. Trust her to appear. "I don't know what you're complaining about."

"Don't forget," Pearl said. "There's a cruise for two for the winner."

"If you win, Jill, you can take me." Grandma was enjoying this much too much for my liking.

"That costume is too small, anyway," I complained. "Look at it! I'll never squeeze into that."

I did. With much pushing, pulling and prodding, the twins somehow managed to get me into it. They then collapsed in a heap, and laughed uncontrollably.

"That isn't helping." I could just about move my arms and legs. The only way I could see was through a small slot cut into the front.

"Let's have a photo of the three of you together." Aunt Lucy and Lester had arrived to see us off.

Amber, the mermaid, stood on my left. Pearl, the princess,

stood on my right.

"Say custard cream," Aunt Lucy said.

Everyone laughed — except me.

In retrospect, getting changed before we set off wasn't such a great idea. Getting a quart into a pint pot may be difficult, but trust me — getting a Jill-sized custard cream into the front seat of Alan's sports car was way more problematic.

"If you put one leg on the dashboard, and the other on the floor, it might work," Amber said, in between fits of giggles.

"No, she needs to put both arms in the air, and one leg on the seat," Pearl added helpfully.

Somehow, and I couldn't say exactly how because it's still a blur, I managed to squeeze into the car. Getting out again on our arrival at the civic hall was only marginally less problematic. But eventually, there we stood — the three of us: the princess, the mermaid and the custard cream. There was only one saving grace, and that was the fact that no-one could tell it was me inside the costume.

"Ladies!" someone shouted. "Photo for the Candle."

The Candle had the largest circulation of all the newspapers in Candlefield.

I thought about making a run for it — yeah right — I could barely walk let alone run.

The photographer took three or four shots. "That's great. Can I get your names?"

"No, no," I said, but my voice was muffled by the costume.

"Sure," Pearl said. "I'm Pearl."

"And I'm Amber."

"We own Cuppy C—the cake shop and tea room. Will you put that in the article?"

"Yeah sure," he lied. "What about the biscuit costume? Who's in there?"

"Don't tell him!" I said to no avail.

"That's our cousin, Jill. She's the one who found the Candlefield Cup."

"The P.I?"

"Yeah. That's her. Jill Gooder."

Thanks girls.

I wasn't sure if all fancy dress parties in Candlefield attracted such a good turnout, or if the prospect of winning a cruise had brought people out in large numbers.

There were all the costumes which you'd expect to find at a similar event in the human world. Everyone seemed to be having a great time except for those who, like me, had made the mistake of choosing a costume which made eating, drinking or going to the loo practically impossible. I spent most of the evening standing next to a man-size battery and a man-size box of matches. Although we couldn't actually hold a conversation, we shared a mutual empathy for each other's predicament.

"This is great, isn't it Jill?" Amber shouted. The twins had spent most of the evening strutting their stuff on the dance floor. Every now and then one of them would come over to let me know they hadn't forgotten me.

"Great," I said.

"Have you seen those two?"

I guessed she was pointing to someone, but I couldn't see her hand.

"There!" She spun me around so I was facing the right direction.

There on the edge of the dance floor was a couple wearing the salt and pepper pot costumes that Aunt Lucy had tried to persuade the twins to hire.

"Do they look stupid or what?"

I assumed it was a rhetorical question, but I was hardly in a position to poke fun at anyone.

"Yeah, what do they look like?" Pearl had joined us. "Do you want to dance, Jill?"

"Yeah." Amber squealed. "Come and dance with us!"

They each grabbed one of my hands—this was going to be a disaster.

"Ladies and gentlemen!" A voice came over the loudspeakers. "It's time to announce tonight's winners."

To my relief the music stopped and the dance floor cleared.

"Third place and winner of a spa weekend is—" Drum roll. "The Comedy Vampire!"

There was only a smattering of applause. I guessed that irony didn't play well among this audience.

"In second place and winner of a hot air balloon experience is—" Drum roll. "Queen of the snakes."

This was a more popular choice. The young witch was dressed as some kind of snake woman with a crown comprised of gold and silver snakes.

"Typical Melinda!" Amber said.

"Same every year," Pearl complained.

I sensed the girls knew the second place winner, and that there was some history between them.

"And so we come to tonight's winner who will receive the magnificent prize of a cruise for two." Even longer drum roll.

"This is it!" Pearl said.

"That cruise is ours!" Amber gushed.

"The winner is — the salt and pepper pots!"

"What?" Amber cried.

"No!" Pearl shook her head in disbelief.

As the condiments made their way to the stage to great applause, I couldn't help but grin. As always, the twins were magnanimous in defeat.

"The whole thing is rigged," Pearl said.

"Someone has taken a bribe." Amber agreed.

Fortunately for me, they couldn't hear me laughing.

Salt and pepper were now on the stage. The MC waited until the applause had subsided before making the presentation of the cruise tickets. The condiments then unzipped the top of their costumes revealing their identities.

"What?" Amber screamed. "I don't believe it!"

There on stage, receiving the cruise tickets, and wearing the costumes that the twins had declined, were Miles and Mindy — proprietors of Best Cakes.

***

Would I ever be able to face a custard cream again after that scarring experience?

Of course I would — in fact I'd just finished my third of the morning. Who says it isn't a healthy breakfast? Experts? Pah — what do they know?

I was considering whether or not to have a fourth when my phone rang. It was Daze — I'd left a message on her voicemail before I went to the fancy dress competition.

"Jill? You left a message to call you."

"Thanks. It's rather noisy your end."

"I've got nine of them today. Oscar is rather excitable."

"Oscar?"

"The Yorkie. He makes more noise than the other eight put together. What can I do for you?"

"This is a long shot, but I may have found your werewolf."

"Really? Where?"

"Like I said, I can't be sure, but someone moved in next door to my sister. It's a man living by himself. According to Kathy, he makes a lot of weird noises."

"That sounds like every man I've ever met."

"True, but she described the noises as a kind of howling, and it was much worse the other night—on the full moon."

"It's still a long shot."

"I know. I thought I'd go over there and take a look for myself, but I wanted to prime you so you can bag him and take him back to Candlefield."

"When are you thinking of checking him out?"

"Tonight, if that works for you."

"Wait until after dark."

"Okay. Stand by your phone, and I'll let you know either way."

"Will do. Oscar, leave Sandy alone. Got to go Jill, Oscar is giving the Pomeranian grief."

***

Before going into the office, I paid a visit to the apartment block where Gina Peel had been murdered. As it turned out I didn't need to resort to magic to get into the building—some kind soul held the door open for me when he saw me approaching. Some people are way too trusting.

The apartment in question was on the first floor. It was easy to spot because it still had police tape across the door. I was considering how best to magic myself inside when the door behind me opened.

"Can I help you?" A middle-aged man wearing matching tartan pyjamas and slippers stood in the doorway.

"Morning." I conjured up my charmingest smile. What? Of course it's a word.

"Morning," he said. I could tell I hadn't won him over yet.

"I'm Jill Gooder. I'm a private investigator."

"Really? How jolly exciting."

Sometimes it worked, sometimes it didn't. Looked like this was a home run.

"Mr?"

"Marlow. March Marlow."

"March? That's an unusual name."

"Isn't it? Momsy thought it would be fun to name me after the month I was born in. Good thing it wasn't a leap year, otherwise I'd have been called February." He laughed. I wondered how many times he'd cracked that same joke.

"Right. Well, Mr Marlow—"

"Call me March. Everyone does."

"Well, March. I'm investigating the murder at the apartment across the way."

"Terrible business."

"Indeed. Did you see anything unusual that day?"

"Wasn't here. I was rowing and getting very drunk. Not at the same time of course."

"Of course. Did you know the victim?"

"First time I saw her was the photo in the Trumpet."

"Bugle?"

"That's the one."

"Who normally lives there?"

"Your guess is as good as mine. Never seen anyone go in the place since I moved in eighteen months ago. Except the cleaner, of course. Must be the cushiest cleaning job ever."

"How often does the cleaner come?"

"Couldn't say for sure. About once a month, I think."

"I don't suppose you know the name of the cleaner?"

"Sorry, not a clue. I did see the sign on the side of her car one day though, 'Spick and Span'." He yawned. "I was about to make some porridge. Would you care to join me?"

"Thanks, March, but I'd better be going."

"Toodle-oo, then."

"Toodle-oo." What? I can do posh.

Chapter 15

I waited until dark before driving to Kathy's. I didn't want
her to see me, so I left the car a couple of streets away.
There were lights blazing in every window at her house,
but next door was in total darkness. I sneaked up next
door's path, keeping as close as I could to the privet hedge
which formed the boundary between the two properties.

Although Kathy and Peter had complained about the
amount of noise their neighbour had been making, the
house was now completely silent. I started by going
around the back. The curtains weren't drawn, so I could
see into the two ground floor rooms at the rear of the
property—there was no obvious sign of life. Either the
occupant was out, or he was in the house with no
illumination whatsoever.

As I began to make my way back along the side of the
house, I heard a knocking sound. I froze. There was
silence, and then the same knocking sound again. I
glanced over the hedge, and there at the first floor
window of Kathy's house was a little face—Lizzie's. Our
eyes met, and she waved.

Oh bum! How was I supposed to explain this to Kathy?

Lizzie had disappeared, and it didn't take a genius to
guess what she was doing. I crouched down behind the
hedge through which I could just about see the window.
Moments later, Lizzie reappeared with Kathy beside her.
Lizzie was pointing in my general direction, and Kathy
was shaking her head. My legs were starting to cramp, but
I daren't stand up until they'd gone. Eventually they
disappeared from the window—thank goodness. I stood
up just as Lizzie reappeared. She pointed, and I could see

she was shouting something. When she disappeared again, I guessed she'd be dragging Kathy outside to prove to her that I really was there.

Time to make myself invisible. I did it just as the door opened.

"Why would Auntie Jill be next door?" Kathy sounded disgruntled.

"I *did* see her Mummy. She's hiding behind the hedge. Maybe she's playing hide and seek?"

"It's cold out here." Kathy complained. Their voices were getting closer.

"Can I come?" Mikey shouted from the doorway.

"No. You stay there. Now, where did you think you saw her?"

"Over there."

The two of them were standing exactly opposite me now — we were separated only by the width of the hedge.

"She was there, Mummy."

Kathy peered over. She was staring directly at me, but I was hidden by the 'invisible' spell.

"There's no one here. You must have imagined it."

"I saw her Mummy. I did, honestly."

"Well, she isn't here now. Come on let's get back inside. It's freezing."

"But Mummy, I saw her."

I heard Lizzie protesting all the way back to the house. Once again I had demonstrated my ability to be the world's most horrible auntie.

***

I'd satisfied myself there was no one home at the

neighbour's house, so I decided to give it another hour or two to see if the occupant returned. For once, good fortune decided to shine on me. A blue Volvo pulled into the drive after only twenty minutes.

From my vantage point behind a large bush near the front of the house, I could hear two voices: a man and a woman. In the dark, I could only make out their outlines, but it was enough to see that the man was at least six-five and built like a tank. I couldn't hear what they were saying, but the woman was doing a lot of giggling.

As soon as they were inside the house, I rushed around to the back. The man led the woman into the living room. They kissed passionately, and then the man poured them both a drink. I felt like a peeping tom.

After only a few minutes, the man appeared to excuse himself, and walked through to the adjoining room. The woman poured herself another drink, and took a seat on the sofa. This was all beginning to look very innocent. I probably should get out of there.

Whoa! I stopped dead in my tracks. The man had begun to transform in front of my eyes! Meanwhile, the woman was enjoying a glass of wine—totally oblivious to the creature in the next room. Then her expression changed to one of horror, and she dropped the glass. The creature, teeth bared, had stepped into the living room, and had his eyes fixed on his victim. She screamed.

I cast the 'lightning bolt' spell which smashed the glass in the patio door. Even then, the woman could not tear her gaze away from the werewolf standing in front of her. The creature had no such problem—it had me in his sights and was already moving towards me. Whoops! This wasn't good. I cast the 'tie-up' spell and the rope wound around its legs. I was taking no chances, so I repeated it twice more. I figured that three lots of rope should do the trick. It rolled around the floor, struggling to free itself. If the look in its eyes was anything to go by, it wanted me dead. The woman was paralysed with fear, which was probably just as well for the time being. I put in the call, and moments later Daze and Blaze appeared—resplendent in their catsuits.

"Nice job, Jill," Daze said.

"Is this your guy?" I gestured to the bound figure.

"It certainly is. You've been a bad boy, haven't you Callum?"

Daze did her usual thing with the wire mesh net, and the three of them disappeared—back to Candlefield where Callum would no doubt be behind bars for some time.

I managed to lead the woman back to my car, and drive her to the address I found in her purse. Once there, I let us both into her flat using the key which was in her bag.

"Look at me!" I said.

She was slowly coming around.

"Look at me!"

When she did, I cast the 'forget' spell.

She looked around—obviously unsure how she'd ended up back at her flat.

"Who are you?" she said.

"I was in the bar. You asked me to help you get home, don't you remember?"

She shook her head.

"One too many shots I think."

"Right. Thanks."

"No problem. Take care. Goodnight."

I had no doubt the woman would struggle to make sense

of the evening. How had she got home? Who was I? There'd be lots of questions, but hopefully none of them would involve a werewolf.

***

I was still half asleep the next morning when Kathy rang.

"What's wrong?" I said.

"Nothing, why?"

"You never call at this hour."

"Look, this might sound like a daft question, but were you at our next door neighbour's house last night?"

"No. Why would I be?"

"Lizzie swears blind she saw you hiding behind the hedge."

"Maybe she was having a nightmare?"

"She was wide awake."

"It's probably all those horrible beanie monsters you've made for her. They're beginning to affect her mind."

"Are you sure you weren't there? You do get up to some weird stuff."

"I think I'd know if I was there. If you must know I was looking through my Vinyl collection."

"When you say looking through them, do you mean cataloguing them?"

"I've told you before. It's much easier to find one if they're in alphabetical order. Anyway, is Lizzie all right?"

"Yeah—she's fine. In fact she's here now. You can have a word with her."

Before I could say no, Lizzie was on the line.

"Auntie Jill?"

"Hi, Lizzie."

"Why were you hiding behind the bushes, Auntie Jill?"
I couldn't lie to my niece. It would be a terrible thing to do. I had to come clean.
"I wasn't. I was here at home." What? So I'm a terrible person — shoot me.
"But I saw you."
"Maybe you imagined it. When I was your age, I used to imagine I had a giant hamster as a friend."
"Yes, but that's because you were weird. Mummy told me."
"Did she?" Thanks, Kathy.
"Come on Lizzie. You have to get ready for school." Kathy had grabbed the phone. "Got to go, Jill."
"I wasn't weird when I was a kid."
"Course you weren't. You and your imaginary friend, Mr Pouches, weren't weird at all. See ya."

***

I called in at the Washbridge office of Love Spell.
"Morning, Nathaniel."
"It's Daniel."
"Oh? I thought you were based in Candlefield?"
"The girls like us to swap around, so we're familiar with both offices. Are they expecting you?"
"No. I thought I'd call in, on the off chance. I was hoping to go through your computer records. Do you think that would be okay?"
"Hilary and Milly are out at the moment, but I guess I could call Tilly or Lily to see if it's okay."
He did, and it was.
Daniel set me up in Hilary's office and gave me her login

details. He also gave me a cup of tea and a custard cream — but only one. Seriously, I knew business was bad, but who can manage with a single custard cream? Still, I had an idea. I finished the biscuit in two bites. What? It was a particularly small one. Then I used the 'take it back' spell and ate it again. It was every bit as delicious the second time. And the third. And the — only kidding. How greedy do you think I am?

The girls kept comprehensive records. There were full details of all their clients: witches and humans. I could see how many dates they'd been on, and which of them had resulted in a successful match. There was one other piece of information included in each date, and that's what caught my eye.

Before I left, I asked Daniel if he'd tell Hilary or Milly that I wanted them to set me up with another date as soon as possible. I wanted to test my theory.

"Just one thing," I said. "Tell them to set me up with a man who they think is my worst possible match."

He looked understandably confused.

"Tell them to find the polar opposite to a match, and arrange a date with him."

"Okay. If you say so."

***

I was in Cuppy C, enjoying porridge (a new line for them) and a coffee. The twins, who'd been busy when I arrived, came to join me.

"Porridge okay?" Amber asked.

"It is, but it's missing a little something." I scratched my chin. "I know what it is. It needs a little salt or maybe even pepper." I laughed.

"Very funny," Pearl said. "You're hilarious."

"We really wanted to win that cruise." Amber pouted.

"It's your own fault. You should have listened to your mum. She told you to go as condiments."

"Don't rub it in. It's bad enough that we missed out. But for them—" She pointed across the road towards Best Cakes. "For *them* to have won, makes it even worse."

"Sort of rubs *salt* in the wound," I managed to say before dissolving into laughter.

The twins sat stony-faced. My humour was obviously wasted on them.

"Anyway," Amber said. "There's another competition, and William and me are bound to win that."

"In your dreams." Pearl countered. "Alan and me will wipe the floor with you."

"Yeah right. You don't stand a chance."

"What's this competition?" I said.

"The Perfect Couple." Amber pointed to the notice board. "Take a look."

I did. It was a format I was familiar with. Couples competed together. One partner was taken away while the other answered questions about them. The first partner then returned and was asked the same questions. The competition was designed to find out how well the couples knew one another.

"So, are you both going to enter?"

"William and me already have. So there's no point in her bothering."

"For your information, Alan and I already have our names down."

"You should come and watch, Jill."
Just try stopping me.

Chapter 16

Suddenly the atmosphere inside Cuppy C changed. Everyone fell silent, and all eyes were on the door.

"What's going on?" I whispered to Pearl.

"It's Ma Chivers," she whispered back.

I was on record as saying Grandma was the ugliest witch I'd ever met. Well, I'd just changed my mind. Ma Chivers made Grandma look positively beautiful. And she was big—not fat—just big. Very big! Like 'don't stand in her way or you'll be bulldozed' big. And where Grandma had a giant wart on the end of her nose, this woman's face was covered in them. And most of them were hairy. Gross!

Everyone stood aside as she made her way towards the table at the back. Trailing behind her were four smaller, younger witches.

"That's part of her entourage," Amber whispered.

After a few moments, the conversations in the room started up again, but everyone seemed to have one eye on Ma Chivers. One of her minions ordered drinks and cakes for the group. For a big woman, Ma Chivers spoke very softly. I'd hoped I might overhear her conversation, but there was no chance. I considered using the 'listen' spell, but figured a level six witch would realise what I was doing.

Pearl checked her watch. "We have to go now."

"Go where?" I had no idea what she was talking about.

"Come on." Amber grabbed my arm. "You'll thank us."

They virtually dragged me along the street.

"Where are we going?"

"Mum's."

"What about the shop? Will it be okay with Ma Chivers in

there?"

"It'll be fine. She's been in a few times since she came back."

When we walked into the kitchen, Aunt Lucy barely registered our presence. She was too busy staring out of the window.

"Make room for us." Amber nudged her mother aside.

There was hardly enough space for me to squeeze in, but when I eventually did, it was worth it.

"He gets better looking every time I see him," Amber said.

"No kidding." Pearl's mouth was hanging open.

The three of them were mesmerised by Aunt Lucy's gardener, Jethro, who was Lutheresque in terms of physique and good looks — not that I'd noticed.

"One man shouldn't be so hot." Amber was almost drooling.

"The three of you shouldn't even be looking," I said, in my most self-righteous voice. "You all have partners. What would they think if they could see you now?"

It was like talking to a brick wall. It was Jethro-time and nothing was going to interrupt that.

Only when Jethro had finally finished his stint and left, did things get back to normal.

"You two should be ashamed of yourselves. You both have a fiancé," Aunt Lucy said.

Amber and Pearl exchanged a glance.

"You can't talk, Mum," Amber said. "You were drooling too."

"I have never drooled."

She so had, but I wasn't getting involved.

"It's a good job Lester doesn't live here, or he might have

seen you." Pearl sniggered.

The twins knew as well as I did that Lester had all but moved in already. I was waiting for one of them to give the game away, but remarkably they kept quiet.

When I got the opportunity, I pulled Aunt Lucy to one side.

"Thanks for taking Barry for the *you-know-what*."

"I thought I'd better. I could see you were a little squeamish."

"It wasn't that," I lied. "It's just—err—that I've been rather busy. You know how it is."

"Oh, I know exactly how it is." She gave me a knowing smile.

***

Mrs V was busy on her laptop.

"No more noise from next door?" I asked.

"Not a whisper. Whatever you did seems to have done the trick."

"Any potential new clients?"

"One man did come in this morning."

"Oh. What did he want?"

"Nothing. He'd taken a wrong turning. He was looking for Armitage, Armitage, Armitage and Poole."

Great. If things didn't start to look up soon, I'd have to make the ultimate sacrifice. I'd have to ask Grandma to give me the benefit of her marketing expertise. Even the thought of it made me want to cry.

"You haven't forgotten about tonight, have you, dear?"

Tonight? What was happening tonight?

"No, of course not."

"Eight o'clock."

"Yes. Eight o'clock. Tonight."

"You haven't got a clue what I'm talking about have you?"

I was so transparent. "It's on the tip of my tongue."

"It's my first studio interview for Wool TV."

"Yes. Of course. Have they told you who it is you'll be interviewing yet?"

"No. I wish they would, but they insist they're going for spontaneity. Don't forget to tune in."

Winky's flags were on the window sill. The cat himself was on my desk, at my computer — as usual.

"I haven't seen you flagging Bella for a while."

He sighed. I was obviously disturbing his creative juices. "Flagging?"

"You know what I mean. Semaphore."

"Bella understands. We're both busy people. As soon as I have this manuscript put to bed, I'll be able to spare her some time."

"So generous. I'm sure she'll be really grateful."

"She should be. It isn't everyone who gets the opportunity to date an award winning author."

"Isn't that a little premature? You've got to finish the book first. How's it coming along anyway?"

"I'm not sure the term 'book' does it justice."

"Isn't it just a story about a wizard?"

Winky stopped what he was doing, and fixed me with a one-eyed gaze. "*Just a story*? What do you mean, *just a story*?"

"Well, it's not like it's a work of great literary merit is it? It's not going to win the Booker is it?"

He gave me a stony, one-eyed look.

"Anyway," I said. "I was thinking. If it does get made into a film, is there a role for an attractive young woman in there?"

"Why, do you know one?" He laughed. "Only kidding. As it happens, there is. The main female character is a young witch about your age."

"Maybe I could play the part?"

"You'd be ideal."

"Really?"

"No, of course not." He laughed. "Why would they cast you when they can have some Hollywood A-lister? A real looker."

"I'm a looker."

He laughed so hard, he fell off the desk.

"You can get your own food," I said on my way out.

***

I found Spick and Span in the Yellow Pages. They had a small office on a trading estate close to Washbridge City Park. I'd tried to call a couple of times, but got the answerphone on both occasions. I'd only been waiting a few minutes when a van pulled into one of the four parking spaces in front of the building. The woman who climbed out looked to be in her late thirties. She had short hair and a long neck. Not a good combo.

"Hi!" I shouted to her.

"Hi."

"I'm Jill Gooder. I tried to call you."

"You should have left a message on the machine."

"I'd rather speak face to face. You are?"

"Brenda Spick."

I smiled. "That's very good."

"What?" She looked puzzled.

"You did say Spick?"

"That's right."

"So, the name of the company? Spick and —"

"Span. Terry Span is my partner."

Was she joking? She had to be joking.

"I thought the names were — err — you know."

She looked confused. "What?"

"You know. Spick and span. As in all spick and span. No?" Just me then.

"Is there something I can help you with?"

"I understand you clean some of the apartments in the East Side development?"

"You mean the one where the woman was murdered?"

"That's right."

"I don't know anything about that. I only went in once a month. The last time was two weeks before the murder."

"Do you have a key?"

"Look, who are you anyway?"

"Sorry. I'm a private investigator."

"I can't help you."

"Just a couple of questions, and then I'll be on my way."

She sighed, but didn't walk away.

"You say you only cleaned the apartment once a month. Is that usual?"

"No. Most people want a clean every week or every two weeks, but to be honest that apartment didn't even need me to go in as often as I did. There was nothing to do — I don't think anyone was actually living there."

"What about the owner?"

"I never met him."

"What, never? What about when you first took on the contract?"

"It was all arranged over the phone."

"What if there was a problem?"

"I had a number to call, but I never used it because there was never a problem."

"Was there anything odd about the apartment itself?"

"No. Apart from the fact that no one appeared to live there. I just did the cleaning according to the instructions, and—"

"Instructions?"

"Yes. The owner was very particular about how he wanted the apartment to be cleaned. I could vacuum throughout, but I wasn't allowed to wipe down the work surfaces or polish the doors. I was allowed to dust them though."

"Isn't that a little strange?"

"When you've been doing this job as long as I have, you get used to weird requests. I've had much stranger."

"Okay, thanks. You mentioned a number. Could you let me have it?"

"I'm not sure I can do that."

"It's really important. It may help to find the murderer."

She looked uncertain, but said, "I suppose it can't do any harm. It's not like they'll be needing my services now."

Once I was back in my car, I called the number. It rang out—there was no answer or even voicemail.

***

That evening I was about to settle down with a good book, and an even better packet of custard creams when there was a knock on my door. Was it Luther? I wasn't ready to face him yet. Or maybe Mr Ivers here to demand his cancellation fee? Or Betty looking for someone to bandage her toe? Maybe if I ignored them, they'd go away.

There was another knock — louder this time.

"Jill!" A familiar voice shouted.

"Jack?" He was the last person I'd expected it to be. "What are you — ?"

"We're here on official business." He had his game face on. It was only when I heard the word 'we' that I realised there was another man standing behind him.

"May we come in?"

I stepped aside to allow the two of them in. It occurred to me that this was the first time he'd actually visited my flat.

"What's going on?" I said.

"We're working on the murder case."

"Gina Peel?"

"No. Anton Michaels." The name rang a distant bell. He was the other person murdered on the same day as Gina.

"How can I help?"

"Earlier today a phone call was made to the mobile phone belonging to Michaels. That call came from your phone."

"From me?"

He read out my phone number. "That is your number isn't it?"

It was. That's when it all clicked into place.

"Why were you calling Michaels?" Maxwell said.

"I didn't realise I was. I got the number from the woman who used to clean the apartment where Gina Peel was found."

"Will she verify that?"

Maxwell had an uncanny ability to really get up my nose.

"Of course she will. Do you think I'm lying?"

"We'll need her details to check." He turned to his colleague. "Bill, will you give us a minute?"

Bill did as he was asked, and left us alone in the flat.

"You didn't have to come mob-handed," I said.

"I'd hardly call the two of us mob-handed, and I didn't realise it was your number until we were already on the way here. So you didn't know you were calling Michaels' number?"

"No. How would I? The cleaner had that number in case she needed to contact anyone with a problem."

"Okay, thanks. I'm sorry for barging in like this."

"What does all this mean?"

"I don't know yet, but it's beginning to look as if these two murders may be connected. Look, I'd better get going."

"Okay."

"I'll call you."

Chapter 17

I was in big trouble. With all the excitement of Jack's visit the previous night, I'd totally forgotten to watch Mrs V's studio debut on Wool TV. It would be the first thing she'd ask when I walked into the office. In desperation I tuned in, and to my relief there were repeat broadcasts of the interview throughout the day. The next one would start in ten minutes. It would mean getting into the office a little late, but it would be worth it to stay in Mrs V's good books.

After the opening credits, the camera focussed on the studio where Mrs V was sitting at one end of a semi-circular sofa.
"Good evening, and welcome to the first ever episode of Annabel's Yarns."
The woman was an absolute pro.
"My name is Annabel Versailles or V to my friends. Once a month I'll be interviewing a leading personality from the world of wool. And just to add a little spice to proceedings, I won't know who the interviewee is until they walk on set. So, let's get the show on the road. Please welcome my first guest."
The camera panned to the left hand side of the set.
"G?"
I could hear the shock in Mrs V's voice as her sister, 'G', walked onto the set and joined her on the sofa. Mrs V took a deep breath—obviously trying to compose herself.
"Ladies and gentlemen. My first guest is my own sister, better known in knitting circles as, 'G'."
'G' stood up and took a little bow to the camera.

Mrs V began with gentle, non-confrontational questions about G's background and achievements. G certainly liked the sound of her own voice, and wasn't shy about blowing her own trumpet.

Everything was going okay until G began to diss Mrs V's own achievement.

"Of course the regional competitions are nothing more than a joke," she said.

I could tell Mrs V was getting angrier and angrier. Eventually she retaliated with a quip about their recent encounter in a speed knitting contest held at Ever A Wool Moment where Mrs V had come out on top.

"You only won because you cheated!" G said, with a smug look on her face.

Mrs V's face turned a shade of red not normally seen in nature. "How dare you accuse me of cheating?"

Talk about train wreck TV.

"Because it's true. How else would you have beaten me?"

Mrs V stood up, grabbed the jug of water on the table beside her, and poured it over G's head. At that point the screen went blank for a few seconds followed by an announcement that this week's show would be cut short, and a documentary on the finer points of purling would be shown instead.

Wow! I hadn't expected that. I'd never seen Mrs V so outraged. She hadn't taken kindly to the suggestion she'd cheated — which of course she hadn't. What she didn't know, and what I could never tell her, was that I'd actually used a little magic to make sure she came out the winner in the speed knitting contest.

***

When I arrived at the office there was a small mobile crane parked on the pavement outside. They were in the process of lowering the printing press which they were removing from the first floor. Gordon Armitage was overseeing events.

"Morning, Gordon."

"Morning." He managed begrudgingly.

"What are you doing?" I said. As if I didn't know.

"Nothing of interest to you."

Now he knew I had no intention of vacating my office to satisfy his expansion plans, he'd dropped any pretence of being civil.

"Mrs V, you're a star!" I gave her a hug.

"Oh dear, did you see it? I was kind of hoping you might have forgotten like you usually do."

"As if I'd forget. I watched it live," I lied.

"I feel terrible for what I did to G."

"She had it coming—the way she dissed your regional win."

"It wasn't that. It was when she accused me of cheating."

"That was a terrible thing for her to say."

"I still shouldn't have done it though."

"I bet it did wonders for the ratings. You'll probably get a pay rise."

"They've fired me."

"What?"

"They said they couldn't tolerate such behaviour, so they've terminated my contract."

"That's terrible."

"I don't mind actually. I don't think I'm cut out for a

career on TV. I'll stick to my knitting and my book."
"Oh well. I suppose I'd better go and feed Winky."
"Before you do, I have a message for you. Someone rang earlier. She said she was an old school friend of yours. Madeline Lane."
"Mad? What did she want?" Madeline Lane, or Mad Lane as everyone had known her back then, had been one of my few friends at school. She'd always been a bit weird, and didn't have many friends herself, but she and I seemed to hit it off. She'd moved out of Washbridge as soon as she left school, and I hadn't heard from her since.
"Nothing really. She said she just wanted to touch base with you, and she'd be in touch."

"Who would have thought she had it in her?" Winky said.
"Who would have thought who had what in her?"
"The old bag lady. She's gone up in my estimation."
"How do you know about that? I didn't have you down as a Wool TV viewer."
"There's a clip of it on YouTube. It's gone viral. She's a star!"

I flicked through the Gina Peel file. It was now obvious the two murders, which had occurred on the same day, must be connected. It was also apparent the police hadn't made that connection until I'd called Anton Michaels' phone. Presumably, they would now open new lines of enquiry. Maybe I should just forget about the case — it wasn't as if I was still being paid to investigate it.

***

Neither Daniel nor Nathaniel was on reception at the Washbridge offices of Love Spell, but I soon found Hilary at her desk. Sitting opposite her was a man in his thirties with tight curly hair.

"Sorry," I said. "I didn't realise you were with a client."

"Jill, wait." Hilary gestured for me to stay. "This is Aaron Knight. He isn't a client. He owns Enchanted. Aaron, this is Jill Gooder, a friend of mine."

Aaron stood up, flashed me a smile, and shook my hand.

"The competition, then?" I said.

"Not really." Hilary stood up and joined us in front of her desk. "We've never really viewed one another as competition, have we Aaron?"

"Hilary's right. There's plenty of business to go around. We work together, and help one another whenever we can."

How awfully civilised.

"Look, I'd better get off," Aaron said. "Nice to meet you, Jill."

"He seems nice," I said after he'd gone.

"He is. He was really helpful when we first set up. I hope you don't mind that I didn't tell him you're a P.I. I didn't want him to think we're paranoid."

"That's okay. I just popped in to see about my next date."

"Are you absolutely sure about this?" Hilary said.

"I'm positive."

"I don't understand. How will going on a date with a guy who is obviously not a match for you help?"

"Just go with me on this."

"Okay, but I think you're crazy. How quickly do you want to do this?"

"The sooner the better. Tonight if possible."

"I'll see what I can do."

"Oh, and just one thing. Can you book a table at a different restaurant this time?"

"Sure."

***

I had thought that taking Barry for a walk was hard work, but it was nothing compared to the task Daze had set herself trying to control the six, no seven, no wait a minute—eight dogs she had in tow. And a few steps behind her, was Blaze with another three of them. I had to hand it to this pair, when they went undercover, they didn't do things by half.

"Hi, Jill!" Daze called while trying to hold on to the pack of dogs.

"Looks like you've got your work cut out."

"It's just as well I've got Blaze to help me. I'd never have managed them all by myself."

"Hi, Jill." Blaze joined us.

"Hi, Blaze. How are you getting on with the dogs?"

"Don't ask. I have a bit of an allergy to dog hair. My eyes are giving me serious gyp." He wasn't kidding. His eyes were red and streaming.

"Thanks for your help the other day," Daze said. "That werewolf had given us the slip a couple of times."

"No problem. I assume he's behind bars?"

"For a very long time." She pulled on the Mastiff's lead. "Killer, stop it!"

"Nice name."

"He's a big soft thing, really."

"I'll take your word for it."

"So, why did you want to see me?" Daze said.

"I spoke to Drake the other day. He mentioned a gang that he thinks his brother might be hanging around with. The Skulls—ever heard of them?"

She had—it turned out Daze had had a few minor run-ins with them over the years.

"Nothing major," she said. "What they do in Candlefield isn't my concern—that's down to Maxine Jewell and her merry men. But occasionally one of them has transgressed in the human world, so I've had to get involved."

"Do you know where I might find them?"

She listed a few of their hangouts, but cautioned me to be on my guard.

I thanked her, and watched the two of them struggle on their way. Such was the life of a Rogue Retriever.

***

Winky was fast asleep when I got back to the office. I sneaked around on tip-toe so as not to wake him up. See, I can be considerate when I want to be.

Then I spotted his smartphone. He'd left it on the sofa under which he was sleeping. I know I shouldn't have, but I couldn't help myself. I sneaked a glance through his messages.

What? I couldn't believe my eyes. He was having some kind of amorous exchange with a female—and it wasn't Bella. Who was Cindy?

"What do you think you're doing?" He snatched the phone.

"Who's Cindy?"

"Never you mind. It's none of your business."

"I thought you and Bella were a thing?"

"We are."

"Then why are you two-timing her with Cindy?"

"Hold on. What business is it of yours who I'm seeing?"

"I feel sort of responsible for you. Kind of like your mum."

He laughed. "You? Responsible? Do you even know the meaning of the word? And anyway, who are you to lecture me on two-timing when you're juggling four men?"

"That's rubbish."

"Okay let's see. There's the accountant guy who I must admit is hot. If I wasn't a cat and wasn't male, I'd—"

"Stop!" I tried to erase the image he'd conjured up.

"Then there's that detective guy. What's his name?"

"Jack."

"How could I forget that? Jack and Jill. Sounds like you two are the perfect match. Then there's the wizard—what's his name? Jake?"

"Drake? How do you know about him?"

"I know everything. And then there's the guy you just went on a date with. Ryan?"

"That wasn't a real date—it was just work."

"Says you. So, I'd say you're hardly in a position to lecture me."

"Okay, let's drop it."

"I'm not sure I can. Maybe I should let each of your men friends know about the other men in your life."

"And how exactly would you do that?"

"Email, text, anonymous letter—take your pick."

"Please don't do that."

"I could be persuaded not to."

"Salmon?"
"Red not pink."
"Obviously."

Chapter 18

Hilary over at Love Spell had confirmed she'd arranged a date for me that night at The Green Wave, a relatively new restaurant which was not far from my flat. In her message, she told me that my date's name was Fred, and added: 'You'll hate him'.

She wasn't kidding. I couldn't understand how he'd ever got through their vetting process, but then maybe there were some witches whose ideal date was a train-spotter who liked to pick his teeth. Fred was the kind of guy I'd have expected Kathy to set me up with. But then, if *I* was disappointed with Fred, it was nothing compared to how disappointed *he* must have felt with me.
"So you've never been train spotting?" he said.
"Sorry, no."
"But you do like trains?"
"They're okay."
"Which one is your favourite?"
"The one which I caught to Llandudno with my sister and the kids was quite nice. They'd just reupholstered the seats."
"I meant *what class*?"
"Class?"
"What class of train?"
That pretty much set the tone for the evening. I've had less painful visits to the dentist, and I felt sure Fred had enjoyed the evening even less. Still, I had to be sure.
"Would you like to get together again?"
He looked at me like I'd lost my mind.

***

I'd begun to think all of Candlefield was picturesque, but I'd been wrong. I'd already checked two of the locations, which Daze had suggested, in search of the Skull gang. I'd seen countless dilapidated buildings and way too many undesirable characters, but I'd yet to find any trace of The Skulls. This was my last chance. Dreadborough, an aptly named area of northern Candlefield was even more derelict than the other areas I'd already visited. At least it was still daylight. This was definitely not somewhere I'd care to visit in the dark. I wasn't exactly sure what it was I was looking for. I doubted they had a sign which read: *'Skull Gang - This Way'*.

I needn't have worried—it seemed they'd found me. Six young men: three wizards, two vampires and a werewolf, all dressed in torn jeans and tee-shirts appeared from nowhere. I was surrounded. They all had the same tattoo on their arms—a skull.

"Hi!" I said, smiling manically.

"What are you doing here?" The vampire with a chunk missing from his left ear appeared to be the ringleader.

"I must have taken a wrong turn. I was looking for the nail bar."

"Do I look stupid?" he barked.

I was guessing he wasn't looking for an honest answer.

"If you can just point me in the direction of the market square, I'll be on my way." I took a step forward.

"Not so fast little girl."

Little girl? I'd give him 'little girl'. I was considering which spell to use to splatter his sorry ass when someone behind me shouted.

"Let her go!"

I turned around to find Raven walking towards us. He was sporting the same jeans, tee-shirt and tattoo as the others.

"She's probably a cop," the ringleader said.

"She's not a cop." Raven walked past the ringleader, and stood by my side. "I know her — she's okay."

"How can you be sure?" the ringleader said.

"She's the one who got the Candlefield Cup back."

The ringleader stared at me. "Oh, yeah. I recognise you now. You were in the Candle."

"That was me."

"Sorry, I didn't recognise you." His demeanour, and that of his cohorts, had done a one-eighty. Suddenly I was the hero of the day. Even hardened gang members enjoyed their sport it appeared.

After the others had left, I sat on a block of concrete with Raven.

"Drake is really worried about you. Why don't you come back with me, and put his mind at rest?"

"I can't." He picked up a stone and skimmed it across the road. "It's too dangerous. I don't want to put his life at risk too."

"Who from? TDO?"

He nodded. "It's my own stupid fault. I let myself get dragged in by that evil cow."

That description matched only one person I could think of.

"Alicia?"

"Yeah. She's pure evil that one. At first she was all

sweetness and light, and like a fool, I fell for it."

"Don't beat yourself up. She had me fooled too, and then she poisoned me."

"You're lucky to still be alive. She doesn't usually let anyone off so lightly."

"So did you get to meet TDO?"

He laughed. "I don't know anyone who has."

"Not even Alicia?"

"I don't think so."

"So what happened? Why are they after you?"

"As soon as I realised the sort of things they were up to, I wanted out. But you don't just walk away from Alicia, and especially not from TDO. I was lucky—I managed to get out, but I still have to keep a low profile. Will you tell Drake I'm okay, and not to worry."

"I'll tell him you're okay, but I'm not sure that will stop him worrying."

"Don't mention the TDO thing, please."

"Okay. Take care of yourself."

***

I checked in with Milly at Love Spell. She confirmed Fred had declared our date an unmitigated disaster.

"That's great," I said.

"If you say so."

"I have a theory which I need to check out. I'll get back to you as soon as I know anything for sure."

The twins could be such good entertainment value. There was the time when they decided to dye their hair so people could tell them apart—only problem was they both went for blonde. Then there was the encounter with Miles Best. And tonight promised to be more comedy gold from them.

It was the evening of The Perfect Couple competition. Considering they were both engaged, it was surprising how little time either of the twins spent with their fiancé. I sometimes wondered if they liked the idea of being engaged more than actually being engaged. Anyhow, tonight both of their guys had been ordered to attend. William and Alan looked nervous, and I understood why. They'd be expected to get all the answers correct or they'd be in big trouble with the girls.

The last time I'd been in Club Tiny was for the Karaoke competition. I'd gone there with Drake. I had considered contacting him about tonight, but I knew he'd ask about Raven, and I didn't think this was the ideal location to have that particular conversation.

The club wasn't actually called Club Tiny although it was indeed very small. Its name was actually Club Destiny, but the first three letters in the sign had been out for as long as anyone could remember.

If Aunt Lucy and Lester had been taking part, my money would have been on them, but they'd said they didn't want to show the twins up. That had made me laugh; Amber and Pearl hadn't found it so amusing. They were both convinced they were going to win.

Hmm, we'd see.

The compère for the evening was a vampire named Mike Holder. He was wearing more make-up than any of the women in the club. There was a glass booth on the left hand side of the stage. One of the partners sat in there, blindfolded with ear phones on, while the other answered questions. Then the person in the booth was brought out to answer the same questions. The answers were supposed to match—oh dear.

Amber and William were the first from our table to be called to the stage. After the usual meaningless small talk, William was despatched to the glass booth.

"Okay, Amber," Mike said. "Your first question: What were you wearing the first time you met William?"

"My blue and white polka dot dress," she answered confidently.

"And what was he wearing?"

"Black jeans and a white tee-shirt."

"Who is your favourite pop star?"

"Maxine Most."

"What is your favourite colour?"

"Pink."

"Thank you, Amber." He signalled to his assistant to fetch William.

I wasn't sure I'd ever seen a werewolf look more terrified. He knew what Amber would do to him if he messed up.

"First question: What was Amber wearing the first time you met?"

I saw the relief wash over William's face. He knew the answer.

"Jeans and a yellow top."

Amber gave him such a look, and he knew he'd blown it.

"I'm afraid that's wrong. Why don't you tell him, Amber?"

"I was wearing my blue and white polka dot dress. You've got a photo on your phone."

"Oh yeah. Sorry."

"Second question—"

And that's how it went. William managed to get precisely zero questions correct. Yes, you heard right: Zero questions correct.

Sitting next to me, Pearl and Alan were enjoying this way too much. At least I had the good grace not to laugh out loud even though I was chuckling quietly to myself.

Next it was Amber's turn to go into the glass booth. William answered his four questions, and she was brought back out.

Question one—their answers didn't match.

Question two—remarkably they both agreed that cheese was Alan's favourite food.

Question three—their answers didn't match.

Question four—their agony was complete.

A dejected William and an irate Amber returned to the table. I said nothing for fear of laughing.

"That was really good." Pearl laughed.

"Shut up!" Amber snapped at her sister.

"Well done, pal." Alan patted William on the back. William looked as though he wanted to tear Alan's throat out right there and then.

"Our next couple is Pearl and Alan," the compère said.

"Watch and learn," Pearl said to her sister.

The compère chatted to the couple. Pearl was all smiles, and even Alan seemed to have relaxed. They had nothing to beat.

Or did they?

"Don't ever talk to me again," Pearl shouted at Alan when they left the stage. She was close to tears.

"How was I supposed to know you liked carrot cake?" he said.

"Because I eat it all the time. Are you blind?"

Amber and William had recovered a little, but only because they'd witnessed a performance which matched their own. Both couples had managed to score only a single point.

What did I tell you? Comedy gold!

Aunt Lucy had said we should go back to her house afterwards. At the time the twins had been very keen. They'd assumed one of them would be bringing home the prize.

"Oh dear," Aunt Lucy greeted us at the door. "I don't need to ask how it went, do I?"

"Go on." I laughed. "Ask anyway."

Amber, Pearl, William and Alan all gave me the same look.

"I take it you didn't win." Aunt Lucy led the way into the dining room.

"Not quite," Amber said.

"It was close," Pearl said.

The twins looked at me, imploring me not to tell. So, I thought about it for a moment, and asked myself what they'd have done if the roles had been reversed.

"They shared joint last place," I said. What? Come on, they'd have thrown me under the bus without a moment's hesitation.

Aunt Lucy and I had to take a seat on the sofa — we were laughing so hard we couldn't stand up.

"We're going home," Pearl said.

"Us too." Amber stomped out.

Aunt Lucy jumped up and ran through to the kitchen, and

then came rushing back. I had no idea what she was doing.

"Amber, Pearl! Wait a minute. You've forgotten something."

The two girls poked their heads back inside the living room.

"What?"

"Here you are." Aunt Lucy handed each of them a wooden spoon.

Chapter 19

I was still smiling to myself the next morning. It had been cruel of me to tell Aunt Lucy about the twin's abysmal performance on The Perfect Couple, but come on—it was funny. No doubt they'd give me the silent treatment the next time I went to Cuppy C, but it was still worth it.

"Morning, Jill." Betty said, as she walked down the corridor towards me.

"Morning. I see your toe is better."

"Shh!" She put a finger to her lips.

Before I could say anything else, I heard footsteps behind me. It was Norman the mastermind. He walked past me without a second glance. He had eyes only for Betty.

"Thanks for coming to pick me up," Betty said.

I caught her gaze, and she gave me a wink.

"Put your arm over my shoulder," Norman said, and then began to help the hobbling Betty out to his car.

Betty, you crafty little minx.

***

It was like the good old days—Mrs V was back on the scarves.

"Jill, I think I should warn you I may have upset your grandmother."

"It's easily done. What did you do?"

"Nothing really. It's hardly my fault they asked me to do it rather than her, is it?"

I loved it when she talked in riddles. Especially first thing in the morning when I was still half asleep.

"Who asked you to do what?"

"Scarves Around Washbridge."

There had to be more than that, so I waited. And waited.

"Should I know what that is?"

"Sorry, dear. I spend so much time in yarnie circles I sometimes forget you aren't in the loop. Scarves Around Washbridge is a charity event organised by the Yarn Council. It's in aid of those incapacitated through knitting."

"I hadn't realised it was such a dangerous activity."

"You'd be surprised. Those needles can be rather sharp. I've seen some things. Take Sheila Pearce—her nose may never be the same again. I have a photo somewhere—"

"No, it's okay. So what does this have to do with Grandma?"

"They have asked me to officially open this year's event. Your grandmother is a little miffed according to my Twitter feed."

"Hold on. Did you say Twitter?"

"Yes. Hashtag ScarvesAroundWashbridge."

"You're on Twitter?"

"Of course. The yarnies love to tweet."

It was at times like this that I realised I was being left behind by the digital age. It came to something when my elderly PA and my cat were more clued up than I was.

***

The Bugle had run a story which confirmed the police had now connected the Gina Peel murder and the Anton Michaels murder. I doubted the story had been based on an official police announcement; it was more likely to have come from one of the Bugle's 'sources' inside the police force. It seemed to me that it all revolved around the apartment where Gina Peel had been murdered. Based upon what the plumber had told me, there was a strong possibility that someone had deliberately sabotaged the pipes to get Gina out of her own apartment. The questions were:

- who had given her access to the apartment where she was murdered?
- how were Reg Peel's fingerprints in that apartment and on the murder weapon when he'd died in a climbing accident two years before?
- what was Anton Michaels' role in all of this, and why had he been murdered?

After some research, I managed to trace the property record for the apartment where Gina had died. It had last changed hands just over two years ago—when Anton Michaels purchased it. The owner prior to that was a Ms Sylvia Long who fortunately still lived locally, and who had agreed to talk to me.

Sylvia Long had obviously moved up in the world. She now lived in a large detached house in the leafier part of Washbridge. It was the kind of area where the residents stuck pictures of flowers on their wheelie bins.

"Do come in." Sylvia led me into a huge conservatory which looked out over a beautifully manicured garden.

"Tea?"

"Thanks."

She rang a hand-bell, and an elderly woman appeared. "Tea for two please, Jean."

Jean scurried away to make the tea. Sylvia puffed on an e-cigarette which smelled like the gerbil cage I'd had as a kid.

We made small talk until the tea arrived. In fact, that's not strictly speaking true. Sylvia made small talk—I smiled and nodded at the appropriate points.

"I assume you heard about what happened at your old apartment?"

"I did. That poor woman. It's the best thing I ever did—moving out of there. It's beginning to look as though the place might be cursed."

"Did you know that the person you sold the apartment to was also dead?"

"I did. Such a tragic accident."

"Accident?"

"Yes, it was all over the papers at the time."

Now I was confused. Why would she think Anton Michaels' death was an accident? Unless—

"When exactly was this *accident*?"

"Not long after he'd bought the apartment, so two years ago I guess. Some kind of climbing accident—terrible thing."

"Look, I'm sorry to press the point, but just so I'm clear: you're saying the man who bought the apartment from you was killed in a climbing accident two years ago?"

"That's right."

I took out my smartphone, brought up the web browser and did a search. When I'd found the image I was looking for, I showed it to Sylvia.

"Was that the man who bought your apartment?"

"Yes, dear. That's him."

***

The lunchtime rush was over, so it was fairly quiet in Kaleidoscope.

"Table, madam?" The maître d' greeted me at the door.

"Not today, thanks. Just a quick drink."

He nodded me through, and I made my way to the bar. There was a different man working behind the bar today; this guy was all hair gel and aftershave. I ordered a soda — last of the big spenders, that's me.

"I see you've had a revamp," I said.

"Yeah. Made a good job of it, don't you think?"

"Very nice. What's the new owner like?"

He shrugged. "Never met him."

"That's unusual isn't it? Do you know his name or where I can contact him?"

"No, sorry."

He walked to the other end of the bar, and began to speak to a man in a black suit.

I cast the 'listen' spell, filtered out all other sounds, and homed in on their conversation.

"She's asking about the owner," the barman said.

"What about him?"

"Who he is and how to contact him."

"What did you tell her?"

"Nothing. You said we should let you know if anyone asked questions."

"Okay. You did good."

The suit then came around the bar and made his way over to me.

"Afternoon." His smile couldn't have been any more false.

"Hi."

"Quiet drink alone?"

"Yeah. I just needed to take the weight off for a while."

"Busy day?"

"Very."

"What is it you do?"

"I'm a secret agent."

He looked nonplussed for a moment, and then laughed. "That must be exciting. What do you really do?"

"That's a secret."

"Well, enjoy your drink."

"Before you go. I asked your barman who owns Kaleidoscope now. He didn't seem to know."

The man's expression was one hundred per cent serious now. He said nothing.

"Do *you* know?" I pressed.

"What's your interest?"

"If I told you that I'd be forced to kill you." I smiled. "Secret agent stuff."

"Sorry, I can't help."

With that, he walked away.

I cast the 'listen' spell again, and focussed on the man as he disappeared from sight. Moments later my hunch paid off as I heard him make a call.

"Some woman. I don't know. No, of course I didn't tell her. Okay. Yes, I'll see you tomorrow at eleven."

Bingo!

***

It was time to face the music. I didn't think I'd be the twin's favourite person after telling Aunt Lucy about their performance at The Perfect Couple competition. Looking back now, maybe I shouldn't have done it. Who was I kidding? I'd do it again in a heartbeat.

"Look who it isn't." Pearl shot me a look.

"It's the traitor, herself." Amber joined her sister behind the counter.

"Look girls, I'm truly sorry." I lied. "But you would have done the same to me."

They looked at one another, and could no longer maintain their annoyed expressions.

"You're right." Amber giggled.

"Yeah—we'd have given you up in a flash." Pearl smiled.

"So am I forgiven?"

"Yeah, we forgive you, but we haven't forgiven those guys."

By 'those guys' I assumed they meant Alan and William.

"Pearl and I spent ages analysing where we'd gone wrong," Amber said.

"Yeah." Pearl took over. "We realised we weren't at fault. It was the guys who let us down."

I nodded, but that wasn't how I remembered it. I seemed to recall that none of them had known anything about one another.

"You're totally right," I said. What? Sometimes hypocrisy is the better part of valour.

"Anyway." Pearl took a bite from the first half of her 'reduced-calorie' muffin. "We have other things on our minds right now."

Make-up? Dresses? Jethro?

Amber stole a bite of Pearl's muffin, much to her sister's annoyance. "Have you heard about the new tea room that's opening?"

News travelled fast. I hadn't been sure whether to tell them about Grandma's tea room or not.

"Grandma told you then?"

"Told us what?"

"About the tea room."

"How would she know about it?"

Conversations with the twins could sometimes be a challenge. This was looking like one of those times.

"Now, I'm confused," I confessed. "I thought you were annoyed because Grandma is opening a tea room."

"She's doing what?" Pearl practically spat out her muffin.

"Grandma?" Amber looked shell-shocked.

"Isn't that what you were talking about?"

"No. We're talking about the two 'M's."

It took a few seconds for it to click, but then I realised they were referring to Miles Best and Mindy Lowe who ran Best Cakes. I glanced out the window, and saw that there were workmen in the building adjacent to the cake shop.

"When did you find out?" I asked.

"Miles had the barefaced cheek to come over here and announce it. He said he wanted us to hear it from him first. And that he knew we'd welcome the competition."

"And what did you say?"

"It isn't repeatable."

Oh dear. It seemed the cake wars had escalated.

"What's this about Grandma?" Pearl scooped up the last few crumbs of muffin.

"She's taken the shop next to Ever A Wool Moment, and is going to turn it into a tea room for the yarnies. I have my suspicions that she used magic to drive the previous tenant out, but I can't prove it."

"Sounds like the type of thing she'd do," Amber said.

"What does she know about running a tea room?" Pearl rolled her eyes.

"Not much probably," I said. "But I wouldn't bet against

her making a success of it. If Ever A Wool Moment is anything to go by, we know she has the marketing nous."

"Just as long as she doesn't try to drag us into it." Pearl stood up.

"I hadn't thought of that." Amber looked at her sister. "Do you think she'll ask us for help?"

"She can ask all she wants."

"Yeah. Let her ask. We'll tell her we're too busy."

"Yeah."

Brave words indeed.

Chapter 20

I was in the office snatching some computer time while Winky was having a nap.

Mrs V popped her head in the door and said, "That friend of yours is here, Jill."

"Friend?" Like I had that many.

"The one from your school days. I mentioned she called the other day. Is it convenient?"

Madeline Lane, or Mad Lane as everyone used to know her, was the original wild child. It was strange that we'd been friends because I'd been a quiet, reserved child. No one could accuse Mad of that. And the clothes she wore: skirts barely longer than a belt, and tops that showed way too much cleavage. Mrs V was hiding it well, but would no doubt have something to say about her appearance after Mad left.

"Show her in."

"Jill." Mad's voice was the same, but it was the only thing that was.

"Mad?"

"It's Madeline now. I dropped the nickname."

"Madeline. You — err — you look — "

"You look great, Jill. You've hardly changed at all."

I couldn't say the same for her. Gone were the racy, outrageous clothes. In their place was a woollen two piece. Her grey blouse was buttoned up to the neck; her skirt was several inches below the knee. And her wild hair was in a tight bun.

"Sit down." I hoped I didn't sound as stunned as I felt. "It's good to see you again."

"You too." She glanced around the room. "Is this your dad's old place?"

"Yeah. I took over the family business after he died."

"I was sorry to hear about your mum and dad. They were nice people."

Mad—err—Madeline had spent many an hour at my house. Mum and Dad had always welcomed her, even if they hadn't approved of the way she dressed. They probably figured I didn't have many friends, so they daren't risk chasing any of them away.

"When did you come back to Washbridge?"

"A couple of weeks ago. It hasn't changed very much."

"You have."

"Yeah well. It was time I grew up and put all of the wildness behind me."

"So are you back for good? Have you got a job? Where are you living?"

"Looks like I might be back to stay. I have a small flat over by Broom's Park—as far away from my folks as I could get."

She smiled, but I thought she probably meant it. She hadn't had the best of relationships with her parents.

"I've got a job at the library."

"A librarian?" That explained the outfit, but not the total transformation.

"Surprised?"

"A little. I have to be honest; I didn't have you down as a librarian."

"Neither did I. But here I am. Does Kathy still live around here?"

"Yeah. Her and Peter have two kids now."

"What about you? Are you married?"

"Me? No. Still free and single. What about you?"
She hesitated. "I'm single now too."
I thought she was going to say more, but she seemed to think better of it.
"We'll have to go out some time," I said.
"Yeah. I'd like that."

What a very nice young lady," Mrs V said after Madeline had left.
"Yeah. She's changed so much. I'm not sure I'd have recognised her if I'd met her in the street."
Winky was still asleep—he hadn't stirred even while Madeline was in the office—writing obviously took its toll. I thought back to how Madeline used to be, and how much she'd changed. As a kid, she'd been a bit weird—that's probably why we hit it off. If I remembered correctly, she'd had imaginary friends she used to talk to. But then, everyone has their little eccentricities, I guess—except me, obviously.

***

The manager at Kaleidoscope left the restaurant on foot at a quarter to eleven. I'd been watching from the store across the road for the last thirty minutes. He looked to be wearing the same suit as he'd worn the last time I'd seen him. I crossed the road and tucked in about twenty metres behind him. He stopped at a small newsagent, picked up a bar of chocolate, and then carried on. Judging by the way the buttons on his jacket were straining, he could have done without the calories.
As he passed the launderette where Daze had once

worked, he took a left. I held back to be sure he didn't double back, and then I peeped around the corner of the building. I did so just in time to see him go through a door which appeared to be the entrance to the offices directly above the launderette. I hurried down the alley and tried the door. It was locked. There was no sign to indicate who the office belonged to, and no bell to ring. I hurried back up the alley, and into the launderette.

"Excuse me," I said to the woman who was sitting on a stool in the corner, reading a book. "Do you know if there's another way into the offices above your shop? I've managed to lock myself out."

"There's a fire escape around the other side of the building. I imagine that would get you up there."

"Would you mind letting me go through to it?"

She gave me the once over, and must have decided I looked harmless enough. "Come with me."

The steel fire escape had seen better days, and made one heck of a row with every step I took. I might have been better using the 'levitation' spell, but that would have taken some explaining to the woman who was still standing on the ground below me—watching my every step.

"I'm okay now," I said, as loud as I dared.

"Okay dear."

Once she'd disappeared back inside I made my way to first floor level. I didn't bother trying the door—I was pretty sure it would be locked too. Instead, I edged along the platform, and leaned forward so I could see inside. Standing at the far side of the room with his back to me, was the man from Kaleidoscope. He was obviously talking to someone seated behind the desk, but my view of the other man was obscured.

Suddenly the voices inside became raised. I couldn't hear what they were saying, but it was obvious they were arguing. Just then the man behind the desk stood up, and banged his fist down. I could see him clearly now.

I pulled back from the window, and hurried back down the fire escape—I'd seen all I needed to see.

I spoke to Hilary at Love Spell, and arranged to meet with all of the girls at Cuppy C that evening.

***

My phone rang. It was Kathy.

"I'm going to strangle that woman," she yelled.

"Who?"

"Your grandmother!"

Quelle surprise! I'd wondered how long the honeymoon would last. It sounded as though it was well and truly over now.

"What has she done?"

"She must think I'm some kind of super woman. Did you know she's opening a tea room next door to Ever?"

"I had heard something about it."

"Well guess who she expects to oversee the building work?"

It was a rhetorical question, I was sure.

"Muggins here—that's who. And not just that. I'm also supposed to be overseeing the Everlasting Wool promotion, and handling the queries which come from the web site."

"That does sound like a lot for one person."

"You're not kidding. How am I supposed to do all that?

I'm going to ask her if she wants me to stick a broom up my—"

"I get the picture. I did warn you."

"I know you did. I should have listened."

"Hang on. Are you actually saying I was right?"

"Yes, you were right. Now what am I supposed to do? You seem to know how to handle her. What should I do?"

"Me? Don't ask me. I have no idea."

"Come on, Jill, please. You're the only person she seems to take any notice of."

"Threats are the only thing that work with Grandma."

"What do you mean?"

"I mean it's no good trying to be reasonable or conciliatory. She'll walk right over you. You need to go to her, and tell her that unless she takes some of the work off you, you'll resign."

"But I need this job."

"She won't let you leave. You're doing too good a job."

"Why thank you, sis."

"Tell her straight. She'll probably huff and puff, and might even threaten to let you go, but if you stand your ground, she'll make some compromises."

"Okay. I'll give it a try. Thanks."

What had I done? What if I'd got it wrong and Grandma did fire Kathy? My life wouldn't be worth living. Even worse, what if she turned her into a cockroach, or a slug?

***

I arrived at Cuppy C before the girls from Love Spell. The twins were taking down the 'cupcake guarantee' sign.

"What's going on?" I said, as I eyed the blueberry muffins.

"We've had to abandon this idea." Pearl unhooked her side of the banner.

"Really? I thought it was one of your better initiatives."

"We didn't take into account those three." Pearl gestured to the corner table. I hadn't noticed Grandma who was sitting there with two of her cronies. Talk about the three ugly sisters.

"What's she done now?"

"They've been here for almost three hours. They bought one cupcake each when they came in. Since then they keep coming back to the counter, and saying the cupcake hasn't made them happy. Then they demand another one."

I glanced across at the motley crew. "Nothing could make those three happy."

"I know." Amber began to roll up the banner. "Grandma knows very well that's not what the guarantee means, but she insists that until she's happy, she's entitled to free cupcakes."

"You'll be waiting a long time until *she's* happy."

"Well the sign's gone now, so the next time they come to the counter, they can just whistle," Pearl said in a whisper.

As if on cue, Grandma and the other two ugly sisters stood up, and made their way to the exit. Grandma seemed to remember something, and headed back to the counter.

"The sign is down," Amber managed meekly. "You can't have any more cupcakes."

Pearl and I both stared at her—she'd obviously lost her mind.

"That's okay, dear," Grandma said. "We've had our fill. I

just came over to give you and your sister some good news."

The twins looked terrified, and understandably so.

"I've decided to allow you to train my staff when my tea room opens."

"*Allow* us to?" Pearl said.

"No need to thank me," Grandma said. "I'll let you know when I need you."

Neither of the twins spoke until they were absolutely sure Grandma had gone.

"Train her staff? I don't think so," Pearl said.

"No way are we training her staff." Amber huffed.

"Jill." Pearl turned to me. "You have to tell her we're not going to do it."

"Me? Don't drag me into it."

"But she likes you."

"Oh, yeah. She's crazy about me."

"Please, Jill."

"Please!"

"Okay. Let me think about it." I took a moment. "I've thought about it, and the answer is no."

The twins were still muttering under their breath when the girls from Love Spell arrived.

"What's wrong with the twins?" Lily asked as she brought the tray of drinks and muffins—blueberry yay!—over to the table.

"Grandma is causing them grief as usual."

"I always thought your grandmother was kind of sweet," Tilly said.

Sweet? This woman was obviously in need of urgent psychiatric help.

"Okay. I think I may know what caused the recent downturn in successful matches," I said.

The girls were all ears.

"I spent a lot of time going through your records, and ran numerous different analyses over the figures. One thing in particular stood out for me. The percentage of overall successful matches is actually as high now as it has ever been, but only at two out of three restaurants which you use for the initial date. Almost all of the unsuccessful dates had their first date at Kaleidoscope. I became suspicious after my date there. Now, my love life may be a train wreck, but I know the date with Ryan went fine. When I left him that night he was keen that we should meet up again. And yet, his report back to you said quite the opposite. That's why I asked for the second date. I needed to date someone who I knew was a complete mismatch to check that I could still recognise what a 'bad' date felt like. My date with Fred proved to me that I hadn't been delusional—the first date had been a resounding success. There was no reason why Ryan should have said otherwise.

It's my belief that something is happening at Kaleidoscope. I think that magic is being used to affect the perception of the men. It's probably something in their food or their drink. I'm not sure."

"That's a pretty wild accusation," Hilary said. "Why would anyone at Kaleidoscope want to do that?"

"The restaurant had a new owner about six months ago. Around about the same time that you started to see problems. The new owner is deliberately keeping a low profile, but I managed to track him down. It's someone you all know." I paused for dramatic effect. "Aaron Knight, from Enchanted, is the new owner of Kaleidoscope."

"What?" Milly said.

"Are you sure?" Lily looked shocked.

"I'm absolutely positive."

"That conniving, little rat!" Tilly thumped the table. "Just wait until I get my hands on him!"

Chapter 21

The door to my office burst open, and in stormed Grandma. She did not look happy.

"I'm not happy," she said.

See, what did I tell you? Can I read that woman or what? Hot on her heels was Mrs V.

"Sorry, Jill. I did try to tell her that she'd have to wait until I'd checked you were free."

"I do not need permission to speak to my granddaughter, thank you very much."

Mrs V looked at me and I nodded. "It's okay."

Mrs V left us alone, and Grandma fixed me with her gaze.

"Good morning, Grandma," I said, trying to sound bright and breezy.

"There is nothing *good* about this morning."

"Right—okay. So what exactly seems to be the problem?"

"The *problem*, young lady, is *you*."

"And what, exactly, did I do this time?"

"It's not so much what you *did*, as much as what you *haven't done*."

"Okay—what haven't I done?"

"You haven't progressed to level three yet."

"Huh?"

"Sorry, am I speaking too fast for you? I said, 'you—haven't—progressed—to—level—three—yet'."

"But I've only just become a level two witch. The twins have known they were witches since they were born, and they're still only on level two."

"I'm not talking about the twins. I'm talking about you. You are your mother's daughter. Darlene was a level six witch. I'm a level six witch. By now, you should be knocking on the door to becoming one yourself."

"Just a minute. If I'd known I was a witch since the time I was born, maybe I would have been further up in the levels, but I—"

"Don't argue with me, young lady. The fact is: you are still on level two, and it is not good enough. I want you on level three within the next few weeks, or I will want to know why."

"But, Grandma—"

"Don't argue with me. Just get it done."

With that, she turned around, crashed back out the door, and disappeared. Where had that come from? The last time I'd seen her, she'd seemed to think I was doing okay. Now, suddenly, I was a slacker. It didn't make sense. Something must have happened, but I had no idea what.

"Don't worry about it, Jill."

I turned around to see my mum's ghost standing there.

"What was that all about?" I asked.

"Ma Chivers has got her riled. You've heard about Ma Chivers, I assume?"

"Yeah, the twins told me a little about her when I saw her in Cuppy C. She looks scary. Even more so than Grandma, and I didn't think that was possible."

"Ma Chivers is a nasty piece of work, but she's also an extremely powerful witch. She's probably the only witch who can give Grandma a run for her money. Fortunately she's been living in the human world for decades, so it hasn't really been a problem. But now she's back, and it looks as though she may be here to stay. She knows just how to wind Grandma up. Ma Chivers has probably been chiding her. She's coached a number of witches, several of whom have reached level five, and at least one has reached level six. Grandma has never really had anyone to coach until now."

"What about the twins?"

My mum laughed. "Seriously, Jill? You know what the twins are like. I love those girls to bits, but as witches they make good bakers. They're never going to be more than level two witches. They don't have it in them and, in all honesty, they're not interested. They like their tea room, they love their fiancés and they love shopping for clothes, but they're really not interested in their witch studies."

"What makes you think I can do it? I'm still new to this. I'm still trying to find my way around the whole witch thing."

"You know you can do it, and I certainly know you can. The problem is that Grandma knows you can too, and she isn't blessed with patience. Before Ma Chivers came back it wasn't such a problem, but now she's on the scene, Grandma is going to be on your case. You've got to resist any pressure she puts on you."

"That's easier said than done."

"It's not going to be easy, but I'll try to help you. So will Lucy. You can't rush these things. You're doing really well, and the pace you've set for yourself is the right one. You'll just have to accept that every now and then Grandma is going to have an outburst like this. You'll just have to learn how to brush it off."

"Did you actually see her just now? I thought she was going to turn me into a donkey or something."

"Grandma wouldn't do anything to harm you. She may get in your face. She may shout at you and be generally nasty, but she would never do anything to harm you. You are her one hope. You are the one witch who can make her proud, and she knows that."

"Okay, I'll try not to let her get to me, but it's not going to be easy."

"Nothing to do with Grandma is ever easy."

***

Dot Comm hadn't been enthusiastic about meeting with me, but in the end she'd agreed. I ordered coffee for both of us, and we took a seat in a quiet corner at the back of the shop.

"Thanks for seeing me again," I said.

"I was surprised to get the call from your P.A. As far as I'm concerned this is now all over and done with. The police have released Reg. After the exhumation, there's obviously no evidence for them to proceed further. I just hope they're actually doing something about finding Gina's killer."

"Look, I know I'm off the case, but there are still some things which are bugging me. I'd like to talk those through with you if that's okay?"

"I suppose."

"I'm curious about how you and Ron came to be with one another because obviously you'd once been engaged to his brother."

"Even when Reg and I were together, I knew that Ron was attracted to me. I realise that must sound conceited, but it's true. I could tell by the way he looked and spoke to me. If I'm honest, I was flattered, and I used to flirt with him sometimes. That was all it was though, it would never have gone any further. Then after Reg died, Ron and I helped each other through that difficult time. I don't really remember when it happened, but gradually we grew closer, fell in love and became an item. It was difficult because I was conscious that some people disapproved, but it felt right."

"The reason I asked you to meet me today is because I've discovered something which I thought you should know, and I'd be interested in your comments. I've spoken to the previous owner of the apartment where Gina was murdered. She told me that the person who bought the apartment from her had subsequently died in a climbing accident. She'd seen an article in a newspaper about his death."

"Reg never bought an apartment; he would have told me."

"Maybe he didn't. Maybe it wasn't Reg. I showed her a photo of Ron which had been in the local paper recently. When I showed it to her, she confirmed it was the guy who bought the apartment. Of course, she didn't realise, and I didn't tell her, that he had an identical twin."

Dot Comm gave me a puzzled look. "I don't really understand what you're saying. Do you mean that the apartment where Gina died belongs to Ron?"

"Officially it belongs to a man called Anton Michaels. He was listed as the owner of the property, but he was not the person who the previous owner had dealt with. Anton Michaels was murdered on the same day as Gina. There's obviously some connection. The previous owner thought she'd sold the property to Reg Peel, but I'm beginning to wonder if she actually sold it to Ron."

After a few moments Dot said, "Are you saying what I think you're saying? Are you suggesting that Ron had something to do with Gina's death?"

"I don't know. I think it's a possibility, but it may be even worse than that."

"No. No, you can't mean—" The colour drained from her face. "You can't think that Ron had anything to do with *Reg's* death?"

I put my hand on hers.

"Look, Dot. I know this is a shock, and it's quite possible that I've got it completely wrong. But the fact is, two years ago, either Ron or Reg bought the apartment where their sister was eventually to be murdered. That property has been held in the name of Anton Michaels ever since. Gina and Anton Michaels were murdered on the same day. Gina was only in that apartment because her own place was flooded. I've spoken to the plumber; he said he thought the damage to Gina's apartment could have been caused deliberately. It seems likely that someone may have done it in order to get her to the apartment where she would meet her fate."

Dot looked totally stunned. I hadn't been sure how she would take this revelation. I thought she might have been angry and upset. I thought she might have told me I must be imagining things. Instead, the look on her face was one of fear. She was afraid that there may be some truth in what I had said.

"What am I meant to do now?" she said, trying to hold back the tears.

"I'd like you to try and find anything which might connect Ron to Anton Michaels. That's the missing link at the moment. If there *is* anything to connect Ron with Anton Michaels, then—" I hesitated.

"It's just too horrible to think about. You're suggesting that Ron killed Reg. That is what you're saying, isn't it?"

"It's a possibility. Maybe it was the only way he could be with you."

"Oh no, I couldn't bear the thought that Reg died because of me."

Her tears began to flow again.

The next few minutes passed slowly as Dot fought to compose herself. She agreed to search through Ron's paperwork, but said it wouldn't be easy because he was with her most of the time. Even when he went out, she wasn't sure where he kept his papers. However, she seemed determined to get at the truth, and she promised to do what she could. Part of me hoped that I'd got it totally wrong because if my suspicions were proved correct, Dot might never recover.

Chapter 22

I could see movement through the glass; there was someone in the outer office. I wasn't expecting anyone, so it was probably a salesman. They would get short shrift from Mrs V, and if they didn't take the hint, the knitting needles would come into play.

The door to my office opened slightly, and Mrs V squeezed through making sure to close it behind her as though she didn't want whoever it was to follow her. Now I was curious.

"Who's out there Mrs V?"

"It's a bit strange. There are two young ladies who claim to be your cousins. They did tell me their names — err — Sapphire and Emerald, I think. Something like that."

"Could it have been Amber and Pearl?"

"Yes, that's them. Are they your cousins?"

"They are indeed."

What were the twins doing here? They hadn't mentioned they were coming to Washbridge, and they certainly hadn't mentioned visiting my office.

"I told them that you might be busy, and said they should pick out a scarf each, and some socks if they'd like some, while I came in here to find out if you had time to see them."

"It's fine, you can send them in."

She went back through to the outer office, and Winky appeared from under the sofa.

"What did the old bag lady want? I was fast asleep until she came in."

"I do wish you wouldn't call Mrs V 'the old bag lady'."

"Okay, what did the old battleaxe want?"

"My cousins, Amber and Pearl are here, so I want you to be on your best behaviour."

"What do you mean? I'm always on my best behaviour."

Before I could comment, the door opened and in filed the twins. Amber was wearing a lovely orange scarf, and Pearl had a yellow and red one. Both of them were carrying socks.

"Hi, Jill," Pearl said. "Look what your P.A. has given us."

"I went for orange," Amber said. "And I've got matching socks, look."

"Yeah, very nice. Come in and have a seat. I wasn't expecting you, was I?"

"No, we hadn't planned to come to Washbridge," Amber said, taking a seat. "We got a call from Grandma."

"What about?"

"She told us we had to come over and help her with the launch of her new tea shop," Pearl said.

"Did she?" I grinned. "Just remind me, what did you two say you would tell her if she asked you to help?"

"Mm, yeah, well—" Amber said. "We *were* going to tell her that we couldn't, but well—we weren't *all that* busy so we thought, why not?"

"Ah, so it wasn't that you were scared of her then?"

"No, of course not," Pearl said. "If we *had* been busy we would have told her in no uncertain—"

"No, you wouldn't. You wouldn't have told her any such thing. I bet the moment she called, you both came scurrying over here like scared little kittens."

"Huh, no we didn't," huffed Amber.

"We did not," agreed Pearl.

"Anyway," Amber said. "Seeing as we had to come over,

we thought we should come and see your office. It's really nice. It's like one of those you'd see in the old detective movies."

"Yeah, I like it. My dad designed it. I think it's got character."

"Character my backside," Winky said.

The twins both did a double-take as he jumped up onto my desk.

"Hey, you know you're not allowed on my desk," I yelled.

"Quiet, woman. I need to introduce myself, as you're obviously not going to do it. Ladies, I am Winky."

The twins both beamed with delight.

"Hello, Winky. We've heard a lot about you, but Jill didn't tell us how handsome you are," Pearl said.

I laughed. "Are we looking at the same cat?"

"Hey, you!" Winky turned to me and gave me a look. "Shut it."

"You're lovely," Pearl said. "You're quite the most handsome cat I've seen in a long time."

"Oh please."

I'd forgotten that Winky would be able to talk to the twins. Listening to the three of them was quite nauseating.

"So, girls, what brings you here?" Winky said. "Did you come specially to see me?"

"No, but I'm glad we did." Amber giggled.

"Have you come to take me away with you? I'm fed up of living in this scruffy old office. And as for this one — " He waved a paw at me. "She doesn't seem to care about me at all. She insists she isn't allowed to have pets at her flat, but between you and me, I think that's just an excuse, so she won't have to take me home with her. I bet you two girls would love to take me back with you."

Amber and Pearl looked at one another, and then at me.
"Don't look at me. If you want him, you can have him."
Suddenly they didn't seem quite so keen.
"Err—well—we'd really like to take you home with us,
Winky, but—" Amber began.
"Yeah, we'd love to," Pearl said. "But—err—we've got a
dog."
Winky's face fell. "A dog? You have a dog?"
"Err—yeah. His name's Barry."
"Barry?" Winky looked at me. "Is that the dog I smelled
on you?"
"Yes, I told you he wasn't my dog, but you wouldn't
believe me. Barry belongs to the twins, doesn't he?"
I looked at them and hoped they'd play along.
"Err—yeah, Barry's our dog," Amber said.
"Yeah, Barry belongs to us." Pearl backed her up.
They had no choice but to play along. They knew if they
didn't, they'd end up with psycho cat.
"Well, that's just dandy." Winky turned his back on them,
jumped off the desk and disappeared under the sofa.

***

"You can still change your mind," the colonel said. His
eyes were watering, and he looked as though he had a
really bad cold.
"No thanks, Colonel," I said. "I'd rather keep my feet
firmly on the ground. Skydiving is definitely not for me.
Are you feeling okay? You look as if you're a bit under the
weather."
"It's just the hay fever. They've been haymaking at the
farm next door. Don't worry about me. You should be

more worried about your brother-in-law. When I saw Peter yesterday, he looked absolutely terrified. I think he was beginning to wonder if he'd made the right decision. Still, it's for a good cause. The dogs will be grateful to him, I'm sure."

"Look who's here kids," Kathy said. "It's your Auntie Jill. She's too scared to jump out of an aeroplane."
"I don't mind admitting I'm scared. Only a complete idiot would want to throw themselves out of an aeroplane from thousands of feet up in the air with just a bit of fabric and a few strings to hold them up. Anyway, *you* can't talk. I don't see you volunteering to do it. You seem to have *your* feet firmly planted on the ground."
"I would have loved to have done a skydive," she insisted. "But someone has to look after the kids."
"Yeah, of course they do. Like you would ever jump out of a plane."
"I'm telling you, Jill, if I get a chance next year, I will happily do it."
"You are such a liar."
"Well, we'll see next year won't we?"
"Look, Auntie Jill. Look what I've made." Lizzie was pulling at my skirt.
Oh no. What monstrosity was this?
"It's called a donguin."
"A donguin?"
"Yeah, this one was Dad's idea. It's really good, isn't it? Look, the head is a donkey, and the body is a penguin. It's a donguin."
"Yeah, it's lovely Lizzie." I lied.
"We've made lots of these new creatures now. We've even

bought a special glass cabinet to put them in. You'll have to look at it next time you come to our house."

Can't wait.

Just then, Mikey started banging on the drum, which was hanging around his neck. It was so loud we could barely hear ourselves think. Kathy pulled me to one side.

"I meant to say, thanks very much for getting that drum for Mikey."

"Hold on a minute! I didn't buy him the drum. Courtney's mum gave it to him when they went to the seaside. It's not my fault."

"He's never stopped playing the thing since he brought it home. It's driving me insane."

"Oh dear, that's terrible." Snigger.

Just then, we heard the distant rumble of an engine, and all eyes looked up to the sky.

"Can you see anything?" Kathy said.

I scanned the horizon, and in the distance I spotted the shape of a small aircraft.

"Look, it's there!"

Everyone watched the plane as it got closer.

"Is Daddy really going to jump out of that plane?" Lizzie said.

Kathy shrugged. "Yes, I think so."

"How will we know which one is Daddy?" Mikey said.

He'll be the one in need of a change of underwear. What? I didn't actually say it.

"Look for the one with the red jumpsuit," Kathy said. "That'll be Daddy."

The plane was almost overhead now, and I could see figures in the open doorway.

"Look, he jumped," Lizzie shouted.

"That's not Daddy," Mikey said. "Those men are wearing green."

The first volunteer was already descending— piggybacking with an experienced instructor. After a few seconds the parachute opened, and they started to drift towards the ground. Moments later the second pair left the plane. They were wearing blue suits. Once again, after only a few seconds, the parachute opened, and they too started drifting towards the ground. The colonel had had a large target painted on the grass, and the parachutists were aiming to land on it.

"Look, there's another one. What colour has he got on?" asked Lizzie.

"That's Daddy," Mikey said.

"No, it's not. That man is wearing orange."

All three pairs of parachutists were now drifting towards the target.

"There he is! That's Daddy," Mikey yelled.

Sure enough, a pair of red-suited figures jumped out of the plane and began their descent.

"Oh wow! He's done it," Kathy said. "He's actually done it. I thought once he got up there, he'd change his mind, but he's actually gone and done it!"

"He'll be okay," I said. "The instructors know what they're doing. They've done this hundreds of times."

"I know he will," Kathy said. "But I did double-check the life insurance policy last night, just in case."

"You did what?"

"Only kidding."

I looked up again. Something didn't feel right. The other

parachutes had opened after only a few seconds, but the red-suited figures were still free falling. I looked at Kathy, who was staring at Peter. I didn't like to say anything because I didn't want to worry her unduly, but I was absolutely sure his parachute should have opened by now. I was just starting to come out in a cold sweat when the parachute opened. Thank goodness! I took a deep breath.

Kathy shouted, "Something's wrong. It hasn't opened properly!"

She was right. The parachute had begun to open, but seemed to have become tangled somehow. Although they weren't exactly plummeting towards the ground, they were falling much faster than they should have been. Fortunately, the kids seemed to be oblivious to what was happening. They were just looking at Peter and laughing.

After a few moments, a second parachute opened. The instructor must have activated the reserve, but this one seemed to get tangled up with the first one, so neither one of them was fully open. Peter and the instructor were spiralling to the ground.

Kathy began to scream. The kids looked at her, realising now that something was wrong. I had to do something, and I had to do it quickly. I'd used the 'move' spell a few times, but never on anything like this. This was a moving target. The force of the two men hurtling towards the ground would be very difficult to control, but I had to try. I cast the spell, and I focussed like I'd never focussed before. As they fell towards the ground, I moved them gradually to the right, away from the target, and towards the neighbouring field. It was going to be very close.

They landed with a thud on top of a haystack. Everyone fell silent for a second. Then the colonel started to run towards them. We all followed.

"Kids, you stay here," Kathy shouted, but they were running with us.

It seemed to take an eternity for us to reach the haystack, and I was terrified of what we might find.

"Phew, I'm never doing that again," Peter said, pulling a handful of hay from his hair. "That was scary."

"You're telling me." A bald-headed man with freckles popped up beside him. The two of them had landed smack-bang in the middle of the haystack. They both looked a little wobbly and disorientated, but as far as I could tell, they were unhurt.

Kathy threw herself onto the haystack, and grabbed Peter's arm, pulling him towards her. They hugged and kissed. The kids ran up to them.

"Daddy, Daddy, you're okay!" Lizzie shouted.

"I knew you'd be okay, Daddy," Mikey said. "I'm going to play the drum for you now."

***

That night, we were back at Kathy's house. Peter was none the worse for his ordeal, but he said his skydiving days were over. The kids were in bed, and he was reading them a bedtime story. Kathy made us a cup of tea, and handed me the Tupperware box containing my custard creams. I was back in favour, apparently.

"I never want to have to live through another day like today," Kathy said. "I feel like I've aged ten years."

"You look like you have."

"Thanks, Jill."

"No problem. Anyway, all's well that ends well."

Kathy looked at me. "I still don't understand how they landed in the haystack. You saw what happened—they were headed straight for the target, and then suddenly they sort of drifted to the side."

"I know. That was really lucky."

"That wasn't just luck. That was—" Kathy hesitated. "It was a miracle. Something weird is going on here, Jill, and I think you know something about it."

"Me?" I shrugged, innocently. "What do you mean?"

"I don't know, but just lately some strange things have happened, and it's always when you're around."

"How do you mean 'strange'?"

"Like when they were chopping down the tree near our house, and it was going to fall on the kids? You rushed across the garden, picked them up and moved them out of the way."

"Yeah, what's strange about that?"

"I'll always be grateful that you managed to save them, but how did you do it? You moved so fast—I could hardly see you moving."

"You and Peter were so scared that you froze. I wasn't in shock, so I was able to react quickly. That's all."

"It doesn't make sense. And what about the time when you lifted the bus?"

"It wasn't just me. There were lots of us."

"Something funny is going on, and it's been happening ever since you found out about your birth mother. Is there something you're not telling me?"

"Like what? Do you think it's magic or something? Do you think I'm some kind of witch?"

Chapter 23

It was the day of the Elite Competition, and I'd arranged to meet the twins at Aunt Lucy's house. Neither of them looked very pleased to be there.

"What's wrong with you two?" I said. "You look like you're waiting to be hanged."

"We hate the Elite Competition," Amber said.

"Yeah," Pearl agreed. "It's horrible."

"But you enjoyed the Levels Competition, didn't you?"

"Yeah, the Levels is great. Particularly the last one when you took part. All the family goes, and everyone has fun— it's like a carnival. Even though it is actually a competition, no one takes it *too* seriously."

Pearl nodded in agreement. "The Elite is very different. It's really serious. The atmosphere is horrible. You'll see for yourself soon enough. It's very competitive. There's no fun to be had; no carnival atmosphere. We haven't been for a few years, and we wouldn't be going today if Grandma wasn't taking part."

"Would she mind if you didn't go?" I asked.

"What do you think?" Amber said. "She'd kill us if we didn't turn up."

"Yeah, it doesn't bear thinking about." Pearl agreed.

"It's not that bad, girls." Aunt Lucy appeared. "Anyway, I'm surprised you can even remember what it's like. When was the last time you two went?"

The twins shrugged.

"It would probably have been the last time Grandma took part," Aunt Lucy said. "And that must be several years ago."

"Why doesn't Grandma take part every year?" I asked.

"She doesn't feel she has anything to prove. You know Grandma; in her mind she *is* the Elite witch."

I laughed. "She certainly doesn't lack confidence."

"That's for sure," Aunt Lucy said. "Ma Chivers was the only serious competition Grandma has ever had, and she's been off the scene for decades. People know your grandmother is one of the most powerful witches — if not *the* most powerful one. But those same people also have a lot of respect for Ma Chivers. Once she'd signed up for this year's competition, Grandma really had no choice but to do the same. If she hadn't, people would have seen it as a sign of weakness. Your grandmother may be many things, but weak is not one of them."

***

The twins were right. When we arrived at the Spell-Range the atmosphere was very different from that of the Levels Competition. There was a good crowd, but none of the carnival atmosphere. Once again, there were bleachers on three sides of the stadium, but on this occasion there was a tall, steel mesh fence running in front of the seating areas.

"What's with the fence?" I asked Aunt Lucy.

"That's to keep the spectators safe."

"Safe from what?"

"It could be anything. The Elite Competition is a whole different ball game from the Levels. There could be some very scary and dangerous spells cast, so to avoid accidents they always install a high fence to protect the crowd."

Wow, now I was really worried. The crowd was seated in separate areas according to which of the competitors they supported. Surprisingly, Grandma had a large number of followers. Ma Chivers appeared to have just as many, and I noticed two familiar faces within their ranks. Alicia and her skinny friend, Cyril, were giving me the evil eye.

The other two competitors were Felicity Broom and Katrina Corke. The announcement over the Tannoy informed us that in each round one of the witches would be eliminated, until the remaining witch was crowned the Elite Witch of the year.

We took our seats and waited.

"What are those?" I asked, pointing to the five large platforms which had been raised high above the stadium.

Aunt Lucy looked up. "I was hoping they wouldn't have those in this year's competition."

"What are they, though?"

"There's a pen on the top of each platform. Can you see them?"

The platforms were so high it was difficult to see what was on top of them, but I could just about make out the pens.

"What's in them?"

"Well, that's the whole point. The reason they're so high is so that no one can actually see which animals are in which pen."

"What happens exactly?"

"Each witch has to choose a pen. They're labelled: A, B, C, D and E. The chosen platform is lowered to the ground, and the competitor has to deal with whichever animals come out of it."

"But isn't that dangerous? Couldn't someone get hurt?"

"It's very dangerous. There have been some serious

injuries, and at least two deaths that I know of. They're wild animals, and there are usually several in each pen. There'll only be one witch in the arena at a time, and she has to deal with those animals quickly using whichever spells she feels most appropriate. One of the most important rules is that they're not allowed to kill the animals. The worst part of this round is that one of the pens will contain a destroyer dragon."

"A what? Did you say 'dragon'?"

"Yes. Four of the pens will contain animals; the fifth one always contains a destroyer dragon."

"What's that? It sounds terrifying."

"They *are* terrifying," Amber said. "I've only ever seen one once, and it scared me to death."

"Yeah, they're horrible," Pearl said. "They're massive. They've got wings, two heads and two tails, and they breathe fire, and they've got big claws and—"

"They do not have two heads," Aunt Lucy said. "They do have wings, two tails and big claws, and they do breathe fire, but they only have one head."

"I thought it had two heads when I saw it—"

"Well, you must have been dreaming, dear. They only have one head, but believe me, one is more than enough to have to deal with."

"Can't they just fly away?"

"No. Although they still have wings, they've lost the ability to fly. Think penguin."

"Do they live in Candlefield?" I asked.

"Well, yes and no. They live on the edges of the sup world, but you wouldn't normally come into contact with one. Every time this particular round is included in the Elite Competition, one of them is captured, and put into one of these pens. If one of the competitors is unfortunate enough to select that pen, she's in real danger. Fighting a destroyer dragon is a totally different proposition to fighting any of the other animals. Their skins are virtually armour-plated; they're fast and they're vicious. All the serious injuries and deaths in the competition have been caused by destroyer dragons."

I swallowed. "I'm not sure I'm going to enjoy this."

"That's why we didn't want to come," Amber said.

"Yeah, it's really horrible," Pearl added. "I don't know why they do it. It should be banned."

"That's something which gets discussed every year," Aunt Lucy said. "Many sups believe this particular round should be consigned to history because it's too barbaric. But there are others, and to be honest that includes most of the level six witches, who think this should remain in the competition as it's a true test of a witch's power."

I looked up at the five platforms. There were four competitors, so the odds of them picking the one containing the dragon were very good, or very bad depending on which way you looked at it.

The announcer called for quiet, and immediately the crowd fell silent. All eyes were on the four cubicles from which the competitors would shortly emerge.

"Ladies and gentlemen," he said. "Welcome to this year's Elite Competition. As always, I would remind you that the fencing is for your protection. This competition can be very dangerous; there will be wild animals in the arena. Under no circumstances should you try to scale the fence. So, without further ado, let me introduce our four competitors. Firstly, please give a warm welcome to a returning superstar, and someone we haven't seen for many years. Please welcome Martha Chivers."

The cubicle door on the far left opened, and out stepped Ma Chivers. When I'd seen her in Cuppy C, she'd looked scary. Today, she looked even scarier—and uglier. She was wearing the full witch's costume comprising robe and hat, and she looked every bit the wicked witch. Ma Chivers looked up at the crowd, and nodded almost imperceptibly to the section where her supporters were seated. I looked across and saw that all of them, including Alicia and Cyril, were on their feet cheering and clapping.

"Next," said the announcer. "We have one of the most powerful witches in all of Candlefield. Please give a warm welcome to Mirabel Millbright."

The door opened and out stepped Grandma. I'd never seen her wearing a full witch's costume before. She looked spectacular—as though she'd just walked off the set of a Hollywood movie. She was scary with a capital 'S'. Grandma didn't look at, or even acknowledge the crowd, and significantly, she didn't look at Ma Chivers. She simply stared straight ahead.

The other two competitors were introduced, and were cheered on by their respective supporters, who were far fewer in number than those supporting Ma Chivers and Grandma.

Based on all the conversations I'd heard while walking to the Range, it seemed that everyone thought the competition was a two horse race. It was Grandma versus Ma Chivers, and the other two were only there to make up the numbers.

"Round one of the competition," the announcer said, "will

be the pens."

There was a collective gasp from the crowd, and everyone looked at the five pens on the platforms high above the arena.

The announcer continued. "The four competitors drew lots prior to the competition to determine the order in which they will take part in this round. The first witch who will face the pens today is Katrina Corke."

Katrina Corke stepped forward, and even from this distance, I could see she looked nervous, which was hardly surprising. The other three witches left the arena. The announcer then asked Katrina to choose a pen. The whole Range was silent, as the crowd waited for her to choose. She looked at each one in turn. I couldn't begin to imagine how scared she must be. My heart was racing, even though I was sitting in the relative safety of the bleachers, behind a huge metal fence.

"I select pen 'C'," she shouted.

No sooner had she said the words, than the platform began its descent. I'd expected it to be lowered slowly, but in fact it came down really quickly and hit the ground with a thud. Immediately, the pen sprang open and out rushed five huge lions. The crowd went wild with a mixture of excitement and fear, as they waited to see what Katrina Corke would do. The lions circled the arena looking for a way out, but could find no escape. As they came close to where we were sitting, those in the front seats shrank back in terror. After a few moments, the lions seemed to notice the solitary figure standing in the centre of the arena. The crowd held its breath as Katrina slowly edged around in a circle so as not to show her back to any of the lions.

One of the lions suddenly rushed towards her. Her reflexes were amazing. I don't know which spell she used, but it knocked the lion off its feet, sending it flying backwards head over heels until it hit the fence and slumped to the ground, stunned by the impact. The next few minutes were a blur. The lions came at her from all directions.

Katrina kept her cool, and took out the lions one by one using a variety of spells. I noticed that she had 'frozen' two of them. Another one was stunned, and the fifth one simply seemed to lose all interest in her. The crowd gave her a huge round of applause as she left the arena, to be replaced by Felicity Broom.

There was a short pause while the arena was cleared. Felicity chose pen 'D', and she was confronted by a number of very angry bears. They didn't cause her any problems though. She used a number of different spells, and at no time did she ever look to be in any danger. She was soon exiting the arena with the five bears totally overpowered.

That left Grandma and Ma Chivers. The announcer's voice came back over the speakers.

"The third competitor will be Martha Chivers." At that, the stadium erupted with applause. Alicia and Cyril were on their feet waving and cheering.

I looked at Aunt Lucy. "Does Grandma have a chance against Ma Chivers?"

"Of course, but it'll be difficult. They're very similar in terms of power and ability."

"Martha Chivers, please select your pen."

She thought for a moment, and then went for pen 'A'. It landed with a thump, and out rushed five crocodiles. Ma Chivers' response was incredible. She barely blinked, and in less than thirty seconds all five of them had been immobilised, and she was leaving the arena as though she'd just been for a stroll in the park.

Grandma entered the arena to much applause and cheering. Aunt Lucy, myself and the twins were all on our feet waving and shouting encouragement.
"The odds aren't good," I said to Aunt Lucy. "There's a fifty-fifty chance she'll pick the dragon."
Aunt Lucy nodded, and I could see she was nervous which made me even more scared. The whole crowd held its collective breath as Grandma looked up at the two pens. One of them contained a destroyer dragon, and I *really* did not want to see it.
Grandma waited for silence, and then said, "I choose pen 'B'." The platform landed with a thump, and to everyone's relief, apart from the Ma Chivers supporters perhaps, out came five tigers. They were barely out of the pen before Grandma had overpowered them. She did it with such ease that it was almost comical. Both Ma Chivers and Grandma had completed the task with an ease which belied the danger of the situation. Grandma didn't acknowledge, or even seem to notice the applause. She simply left the arena. The results were in: Grandma, Ma Chivers and Felicity Broom were through to the next round.

Chapter 24

There was a short break between rounds, and I turned to Aunt Lucy and asked, "What happens to the dragon?"

"It will be left up there until after the competition has finished, and the stadium has been cleared. Then it will be transported back to where it was captured. I'm just thankful that no one chose pen 'E'."

Round two required the competitors to conjure up a storm cloud, and aim a real bolt of lightning at a target. This was a spell I'd never seen before. I didn't even know what level it was, but I assumed it must be at least level five. I could fire lightning bolts from my hand, and I could conjure up rain clouds, but this was way more complicated. The targets were statues, and I noticed they were similar to the one I'd previously used to practise the 'shatter' spell.

Felicity Broom went first. The cloud appeared within moments, and shortly after, a powerful thunderclap reverberated around the stadium. The lightning bolt struck the statue on its head, knocking it clean off. The crowd applauded, and Felicity stepped aside to make way for Grandma.

She conjured up a storm cloud at least twice the size of Felicity's. The ensuing thunderclap was deafening; my ears were ringing long after it had ended. The lightning bolt hit the statue which disintegrated into a million tiny pieces. We were on our feet clapping and cheering, but as always, Grandma was impassive — almost oblivious to the crowd.

Ma Chivers stepped forward. Her storm cloud was of a

similar size to Grandma's, and the thunderclap was every bit as loud. The lightning bolt destroyed the statue in much the same way as Grandma's had. No one needed to hear the announcement; we already knew that Felicity Broom would be eliminated.

"Ladies and gentlemen, I give you your finalists in this year's competition: Martha Chivers and Mirabel Millbright. The final round, as always, is 'mind control'. The two finalists will try to control the mind of their opponent. The aim is to make their opponent kneel before them. Whichever of the two contestants can achieve that first will be crowned this year's Elite Champion."

I turned to Aunt Lucy. "What exactly is the 'mind control' spell?"

"It's one of the most difficult spells to perform. It's almost like a 'level six *plus*' spell. It enables a witch to take over the mind of another human or sup. In itself, that's not so difficult unless the person you're using the spell on also happens to be a level six witch. If Grandma was controlling my mind or yours, she could do that without a second thought. But to do it against another level six witch, and particularly against one as powerful as Ma Chivers, is a very different proposition. They're very well matched, so this should be—"

"Scary?" I said.

"Yes, definitely scary, but also quite interesting. It isn't dangerous, not like the platform round, but it will be difficult for either of them to come out the clear winner."

Aunt Lucy was absolutely right. As soon as the announcer gave the two finalists the go-ahead, the two witches locked gazes. The only sign that anything was happening was in the eyes of each witch. There was something deep, dark and almost sinister in Ma Chivers' eyes. Grandma had a level of focus on her face I'd never seen before. She was always stressing the importance of focus to me, but I'd never seen this level of concentration. I didn't even know it was possible.

The crowd fell silent. It was as though there was an invisible force field moving between the two witches, as each one fought for control over the other. Time seemed to stand still. All eyes were on the two of them, waiting to see which one would fall to her knees.

"Time is up!" the announcer said after what seemed like an age, but was probably no more than a minute or so. "The time limit has been reached. No clear winner has emerged. As is customary in these cases, I declare the joint winners of this year's Elite Competition to be Martha Chivers and Mirabel Millbright."

There was a moment's hesitation among the crowd, but then everyone stood, and started clapping and cheering. I looked at Grandma and Ma Chivers; neither of them looked happy. The stadium cleared, and we waited for Grandma outside. She appeared after about five minutes.

"Well done, Mother," Aunt Lucy said.

"Stupid rule," Grandma said. "Why have a time limit? If the idea is to determine who is the Elite witch, then the mind control round should have continued until there was a winner. I had Chivers; I could feel it. A few more seconds and she would have been on her knees begging for me to stop."

"But those are the rules," Amber said.

Pearl looked at her sister as though she'd lost her mind.

Amber realised what she'd said, and tried to recover the situation. "It's a silly rule though Grandma, I agree."

"Let's go back to my house," said Aunt Lucy. "We can all have a celebratory drink, and a bite to eat."

"There's nothing to celebrate," Grandma said. "You go and celebrate if you want to; I've got better things to do with my time."

"But Mother, you were joint winner of the—"

"I'm not *joint* anything. There's only one Elite witch in Candlefield, and you're looking at her."

"But, Mother. Why don't you—"

It was too late. Grandma had disappeared.

Aunt Lucy shook her head. "What do you think, girls? Shall we go back to my house and celebrate anyway?"

The twins nodded.

"Count me in," I said. I was hungry and thirsty. Just watching the competition had totally exhausted me.

Chapter 25

I told Aunt Lucy and the twins that I wanted to call at Cuppy C because I needed to feed Barry. I said they should go on ahead, and I'd be with them as soon as I could.

As I walked to the tea room I kept replaying the Elite Competition in my mind, and for the first time I began to have doubts about my future. I loved magic. I loved being a witch, and learning new spells. I had thought I wanted to progress up the levels, to become a level six witch like my mother and my grandmother. But after the events of the day, and after seeing some of the scary things involved, I wasn't so sure. Maybe I should be more like the twins, and be satisfied with remaining on level two. I had no desire to take part in a competition like the one I'd seen today.

***

I was almost at Cuppy C when I heard footsteps behind me. I turned around, and a young witch with vivid, blue hair came panting up towards me.

"I've been trying to catch up with you," she gasped. "Are you Jill Gooder?"

"Yeah, that's me."

"Oh, thank goodness. Your grandma sent me. She wanted me to tell you to meet her back at the Range. It's important."

"What's so urgent?"

"I don't know. I'm just the messenger, and well—you don't question your grandma, do you?"

That was true of course, but why hadn't Grandma just magicked herself here if she wanted to see me? I didn't get it.

"Who are you?" I asked.

"I'm, Imelda. I work at the Range. I'd finished for the day, and was just getting ready to leave when your grandmother grabbed me, and said I had to come and fetch you. I'm going home now; my tea will be ready. Bye."

With that, Imelda rushed off down the street.

Great! I'd been looking forward to a drink, and some of Aunt Lucy's cakes. I really needed to de-stress after watching the Elite Competition, but it appeared that Grandma had other plans. Well, I'd still have to feed Barry, so she'd just have to wait for a few minutes.

"Can we go for a walk? Can we go to the park? Can we go now, please? Can we?"

"I'm sorry, Barry. We can't go just yet. There's something I have to do first."

"Oh please. I want to go for a walk. Can we go to the park? Can we go now? I love the park."

"I know you do, Barry, and I'd really like to take you. But there's something I have to do first. It's important. I'll feed you now, and I'll be back as soon as I can."

"Ooh yes. I like food. Can I have some now? Can I?"

"Yes. I'm going to feed you now, and I'll be back soon to take you to the park."

I left Barry to eat his dinner. Once I'd found out what Grandma wanted, and I'd had something to eat at Aunt Lucy's, I'd come back and take him for a quick walk in the park.

The area outside the range was eerily quiet. I made my way to the main entrance, but it was locked. I saw a smaller door to the right, so I tried that and it opened. The inside of the Range was deserted.

"Grandma," I shouted. "Grandma, it's Jill."

"Over here."

I looked into the arena and saw a figure standing next to the remaining raised platform.

"Grandma, is that you?"

It was dusk and visibility wasn't great. I could just about make out the figure in the distance. It looked vaguely like Grandma, and the voice sounded like hers. I walked past the bleachers, and towards the entrance to the main arena. It wasn't locked, so I went inside and began to walk towards the remaining platform.

"Grandma," I called again. I could see her more clearly now, but she had her back to me. What was she doing? Was this some kind of test, or a punishment? Had I done something wrong again?

"Grandma, what's this all about?" As I spoke, the figure turned to dust before my eyes.

"Grandma?" I was really worried now. I looked around. The stadium was still silent and deserted. What was going on? This had all the hallmarks of TDO. Was it a trap? I wasn't sure, but I needed to get out of there fast. I turned around and started for the gate. As I did, I heard a horrifyingly familiar sound. Pen 'E' had dropped to the ground with a thud. I turned around and came face to face with the most terrifying creature I'd ever seen.

The dragon was almost twice the size of an elephant. Its skin had a metallic appearance. Its neck was long, and it had a pointed snout with a mouth full of razor-sharp teeth. Its powerful tail swished angrily back and forth as it began to move towards me. Its head snaked from side to side, and its green eyes burned into me. It felt as if they were pinning me to the spot.

Suddenly the dragon opened its mouth and let out an ear-splitting roar. Simultaneously, flames shot from its nostrils and hit the ground only a few metres in front of me, scorching the grass. There aren't words to describe how scared I was, but I knew that if I didn't act quickly, I would be dead within seconds.

I instinctively called on the 'invisible' spell. I'd used it dozens of times before, and could normally cast it in seconds, but I was so terrified my brain wouldn't function properly. It took me three attempts to get the spell to work. When it finally did, I breathed a sigh of relief. I was safe now because the dragon couldn't see me. I began to run for the exit, but as I did, I heard its massive feet thudding behind me. It somehow knew where I was. Perhaps it could still see me — or maybe it could smell me. Any moment now those flames would burn me to a cinder. I knew I wouldn't make it to the gate in time, so I had to try something else. I cast the 'obscurer' spell, using as much focus as I could muster to create the largest cloud of smoke I'd ever produced. I could no longer see the dragon, but whether it could still see me or sense my whereabouts I had no idea. I sped off again, but I was still at least thirty metres away, and I had no idea whether I'd bought myself enough time to escape.

When I was only ten metres short of the gate I had my answer. The dragon emerged from the cloud of smoke. I stopped dead in my tracks. This was the end. I'd never make it out now. In desperation I cast every spell I could think of: the 'burn' spell, the 'lightning bolt', the 'freeze' spell, the 'sleep' spell. None of them worked. Maybe I could levitate over the fence — but I knew that would take too long. The dragon was getting closer — I was dead. It breathed more fire from its nostrils, and this time it scorched the grass no more than a few inches from my feet. The next one would hit me. I closed my eyes. This was it.

***

The sensation was like nothing I'd ever felt before. One minute I was standing on the ground waiting to become toast, and the next I was tumbling through the air head over heels, doing mini somersaults as I was lifted over the fence, and dropped unceremoniously to the ground. The fall knocked the wind out of me, but I managed to get to my knees, and I saw that the dragon was clawing at the fence, desperately trying to get at me. Fortunately, the fence was strong enough to contain it, and I was just out of reach of the flames.
"What were you playing at?" Grandma shouted. "Have you lost your mind?"
I was still on my knees trying to catch my breath. "Grandma, thank you. Thank you."
"What were you doing in the arena?"

"I got a message telling me to meet you here."

"I didn't send you a message."

"Someone called Imelda told me to meet you at the Range, so I came back. I thought I saw you standing next to the platform, but then—"

"I didn't send you a message. It's lucky for you that your mother sensed something was wrong and told me. Another few minutes and you would have been dead."

Just to illustrate the point, the dragon breathed more fire through the fence, scorching the grass close to Grandma's feet. She turned to the beast, and cast a spell which made it howl with pain. She repeated the process, and it howled again and slowly started to back away.

"Are you okay?" She helped me to my feet.

"I think so; just a bit winded."

"Come on, let's get out of here. I'll let the authorities know they need to come and see to this creature."

"Okay, thanks Grandma. Thank you so much."

***

Grandma magicked the two of us to Aunt Lucy's house.

"What happened to you, Jill?" Aunt Lucy looked shocked at my appearance.

"This crazy granddaughter of mine decided to fight the destroyer dragon," Grandma said.

"No I didn't," I said. "I didn't decide to fight anything. I was tricked. Someone told me Grandma wanted to see me at the Range, and when I got there the platform came down and the dragon came after me."

Amber and Pearl looked at me wide-eyed.

"Were you scared?"

"I was absolutely terrified. I thought I was a goner."

"What did you do? How did you get away?"

"I didn't. I tried making myself invisible, but that didn't seem to work. Then I tried using the 'obscurer' spell, and that bought me some time, but I still wouldn't have got out of the arena alive if Grandma hadn't come to my rescue."

Aunt Lucy and the twins looked at Grandma.

"Why is everyone staring at me?" she snarled. "I thought there were meant to be drinks. Did you get me here under false pretences?"

"You can have any drink you like," Aunt Lucy said. "What will it be?"

"Well in that case, I wouldn't say no to a drop of champagne."

"I'm sorry," Aunt Lucy said. "We don't have any champagne."

"Well, you did say I could have *any* drink, and I would like champagne. I believe the shops are still open."

Chapter 26

I got a call from Dot Comm. She sounded really upset, and wanted me to meet her at an address which she said was a friend's apartment. I tried to get more information from her, but she didn't want to talk over the phone. I jumped in my car, and was there within ten minutes. I knocked on the door, and I could see an eye at the peephole. Moments later the door opened. The woman standing in front of me was barely recognisable as the same one I'd seen at my office only recently. Her hair was untidy, and she looked as though she'd been crying for a long time.

"Come in," she said, and she led me through to the living room.

"Are you okay?" I asked.

"No, not really."

"Is anyone here with you?"

"My friend, Rita, was here, but I asked her to go out while I spoke to you. Please sit down."

I did as she asked, and she took a seat opposite me.

"I did what you suggested," she said. "I waited until Ron went out, and then I searched through all of his papers. You were right. I found a number of documents relating to the purchase of the apartment where Gina was killed, and the name on all of them was 'Anton Michaels'. It was obvious from those documents that it was Ron who'd paid for the apartment, and he was paying Anton Michaels to pretend to be the owner."

"Does he know you've found this information?"

"Oh yes. I told him."

I was shocked. That was the last thing I'd expected her to

do. If my suspicions were correct, and he had murdered his own brother and sister, Ron Peel was not a man to confront.

"What did he say?" I asked.

"He tried to deny it at first, but it was obviously true. In the end, he just confessed."

"To what exactly?"

"Everything. He said that from the moment he first saw me, he knew he loved me, and he couldn't bear to live his life without me. That's when he decided he had to kill Reg."

"He told you that?"

"Yes. I was a bit scared because I thought if he'd killed Reg and Gina—he might kill me too. But he said I was the only thing in the world which mattered to him, and he would never harm me. He's deluded. He thought I'd forgive him for killing Reg because he done it so we could be together. But, I loved Reg—we were going to be married. How could I love the man who had killed him? I told Ron I hated him."

"What did he say?"

"He didn't get angry. He just looked really sad. He said he was sorry, and then he left."

"Where did he go?"

"I don't know. He didn't say another word. He just walked out."

"Have you seen or spoken to him since?"

"No. I don't know where he is. I think there's a good chance he may harm himself. That's why I called you. I didn't know what else to do."

"Okay, well the best thing you can do for the moment, is to stay put. Does he know you're here?"

"No. He doesn't know Rita."

"Good. Well stay here. Don't go out under any circumstances. If he calls — don't answer the phone. I'll go and talk to the police, and tell them everything I know. They'll send someone to collect you. Okay?"

She nodded.

***

"Well if it isn't my favourite P.I." Jack Maxwell had a broad smile on his face. "And what brings you to see me today?"

We were in our usual interview room.

"I have some information about the murders of Gina and Reg Peel, and Anton Michaels. They were all murdered by the same person."

"And who would that be?"

"Ron Peel murdered all three of them."

"I assume you have some sort of evidence to back up that statement?"

"Ron has actually confessed to the murders."

"Confessed to who?"

"To his girlfriend, Dorothy Comm. She's currently staying with a friend, and she's understandably scared. I told her that you would send someone to collect her so that she can make a statement. I'm fairly sure when you find Ron, assuming he's still alive, he'll make a full confession."

"How could he have murdered Gina when the only fingerprints in the apartment belonged to his brother who died two years ago?"

"It's a long story. The short version is that Ron loved Dorothy, but she was engaged to his brother. Ron planned this in meticulous detail. In fact, he planned it two years in advance. He wanted Dorothy, but he also wanted to ensure that he inherited the family fortune which would go to the surviving one of the three children. He had to get rid of Reg in order to win Dorothy, but before killing him, he bought the apartment in which he would later kill Gina. At some point he must have persuaded Reg to go over to the apartment, and while he was there Reg must have left fingerprints on various surfaces, and also on the knife which would eventually be the murder weapon. Ron then preserved that future crime scene under the supposed ownership of Anton Michaels. The apartment basically remained empty for the next two years, apart from the occasional visit from a cleaner. Ron must have thought two years was sufficient time for people not to make a connection between the deaths of Gina and her brother. Once Dorothy had fallen for Ron, the next step in his plan was to ensure that he inherited the money. He orchestrated the water leak at Gina's apartment, arranged for her to stay at a 'friend's' apartment — the one which he actually owned, and which Reg had visited two years before. Ron killed his sister there, making sure not to leave any of his own fingerprints at the scene. When the police discovered the body, the fingerprints they found belonged to Reg."

Jack Maxwell shook his head. "How on earth did you put all those pieces together?"

"There were a number of clues. Firstly, when I spoke to the maintenance man at Gina's apartment, he suggested that the water leak was not an accident. The fact that Gina found somewhere else to live so quickly was a bit too convenient. It was as if someone had been waiting to step in and help. In fact, Ron had done just that. Then after murdering his sister, I'm pretty sure he also murdered Anton Michaels who was the only other person who could link him to the apartment. When I spoke to the previous owner of Anton Michaels' apartment, she identified Ron as the man who bought it from her. Although she mistakenly thought the photo I showed her was of Reg, the brother who she knew had died in a climbing accident. That's when I told Dorothy about my suspicions, and she was horrified. She searched Ron's papers without his knowledge, and found paperwork linking him to Anton Michaels, and the purchase of the apartment. That's when she confronted him."

Maxwell had the same horrified expression on his face as I had when she'd told me that.

"Why would she do that?" he said. "He could have killed her too."

"That's what I said, but it appears that Ron Peel is besotted with Dorothy, and would never do anything to harm her. He really believed she'd love him all the more for having committed those terrible crimes so they could be together. But of course Dorothy was appalled that he'd killed his brother and his sister."

"So where is he now?"

"I don't know. Dot told him she was going to the police, and he just left. I think there's a strong possibility you may be looking for a body."

Chapter 27

Sometimes it was nice to just sit at my desk and do nothing. Or at least that's what I told myself when I had no cases to work on. I hadn't had a sniff of a new case since the Peel murders. Ron Peel, who had eventually been found alive, had confessed and was now serving several life sentences.

"Hey, daydreamer." Winky jumped onto my desk.
"I've told you not to jump on here."
"It was the only way to get your attention. I've been waving at you from the window sill for the last ten minutes. Goodness knows where your head was at."
"What do you want?"
"Just to remind you that you promised to take me to the darts tournament."
"Did I?"
"You know you did. We've had this discussion."
"Okay, when is it?"
"It's in a couple of weeks' time. I'm not sure whether I'm going to take Bella or Cindy."
"Hold on a minute. I said I'd take *you* to this silly tournament. I didn't say anything about taking your entourage."
"It will only be the two of us. It'll be me and A N Other. I just haven't decided which A N Other it will be yet. It depends which of them treats me best between now and then."
"You do realise this is no way to conduct a relationship, don't you?" I said. "You shouldn't toy with their affections."

Winky gave me a look, and I knew I'd said the wrong thing. Any minute now I was going to get the usual lecture about *my* love life. But before he could lay into me, I changed the subject.

"When will I get my share of the advance for your book and the movie?"

"There isn't going to be a book."

"What? Why not?"

"Writer's block. The juices have stopped flowing."

"Well get them flowing again." In my mind, I'd already spent my share of the royalties.

"You can't rush these things. Do you think Dickens simply knocked his stuff out?"

"Are you seriously comparing yourself to Dickens?"

"Of course not. The man was just a hack compared to me which is precisely why I have to wait until the creative juices start to flow again."

"Well get them flowing soon. I have dresses to buy and holidays to book."

The door opened, and Mrs V sneaked into the room.

"Mrs V? Is everything okay?"

"Shh," she said, as she walked over to the desk.

Winky gave her a suspicious look.

"There's a woman out there, and she's a bit—" She looked around to make sure the woman hadn't followed her. "Well—she's a bit strange, and very scary. And, I know this is a horrible thing to say, but she's really ugly."

"Look, if Grandma's out there, just send her in."

"No, no, it's not your grandmother. This woman is way more ugly than she is."

That was impossible.

"Who is she? Did you get her name?"

"She doesn't have an appointment, but she insists that you'll agree to see her. Her name is Chivers, Martha Chivers."

My blood ran cold. Ma Chivers, here in my office? What could she want with me?

"What do you want me to do, Jill? I don't think I dare tell her to go away." Mrs V said, looking back at the door to the outer office.

"It's okay, you can send her in."

"Okay then, but if you need any help just shout, and I'll call the police."

"Don't worry, it'll be okay."

Mrs V left my office, and moments later in walked Ma Chivers. I'd seen her on a couple of occasions now, but I'd never been this close to her before. Boy was she ugly! Winky jumped off the desk and skidded as he ran under the sofa. I couldn't be sure, but it looked as though he was trembling, which was understandable given the circumstances.

"Jill," Ma Chivers said, as she strode across the room. "Good to meet you." She held out her hand which was all wizened and warty — and she expected me to shake it.

Ugh! What was I to do? I had no choice. It felt like she was going to crush my fingers. I tried to smile, but it wasn't easy.

"How can I help you, Mrs Chivers?"

"Please call me 'Ma'. That's what all my friends call me, and I'd like to think that we could be friends, Jill."

She took a seat, and I followed suit.

"So, how can I help you today — Ma?"

"It's more a question of how I can help you, Jill. I've heard such a lot about you. Some quite remarkable stories. You seem to have achieved so much in the short time since you discovered you were a witch, but frankly dear, you could achieve so much more. I can't help but feel you're being held back. Your mother was a level six witch, and there's no reason why you shouldn't make it to that level too — and very soon. But you'll never do it under the guidance of your grandmother. I'm sorry to have to say this, but Mirabel simply isn't the witch she once was. You deserve the best. You deserve someone who can nurture your natural talents."

I really did not like the way this was going. I had a horrible feeling I knew what was coming.

"And so, Jill, I've decided that I should take responsibility for your development from now on. I think you and I will make an excellent team. What do you say?"

Oh bum!

BOOKS BY ADELE ABBOTT

Witch P.I. Mysteries:
Witch Is When It All Began
Witch Is When Life Got Complicated
Witch Is When Everything Went Crazy
Witch Is When Things Fell Apart
Witch Is When The Bubble Burst
Witch Is When The Penny Dropped
Witch Is When The Floodgates Opened
More coming soon.

AUTHOR'S WEB SITE
http:www.AdeleAbbott.com

FACEBOOK
http://www.facebook.com/AdeleAbbottAuthor

MAILING LIST
(new release notifications only)
http:/AdeleAbbott.com/adele/new-releases/

Printed in Great Britain
by Amazon